The Mudfog Papers

Charles Dickens

ALMA CLASSICS
an imprint of

ALMA BOOKS LTD
3 Castle Yard
Richmond
Surrey TW10 6TF
United Kingdom
www.almaclassics.com

The Mudfog Papers first published as a single volume in 1880
This edition first published by Alma Books Ltd in 2014
Reprinted 2017

Cover design © Marina Rodrigues

Background material © Alma Books Ltd

Printed and bound by CPI Group (UK) Ltd, Croydon, CR0 4YY

ISBN: 978-1-84749-348-4

Contents

Charles Dickens (1812–70)

John Dickens,
Charles's father

Elizabeth Dickens,
Charles's mother

Catherine Dickens,
Charles's wife

Ellen Ternan

1 Mile End Terrace, Portsmouth, Dickens's birthplace (above left),
48 Doughty Street, London, Dickens's home 1837–39 (above right)
and Tavistock House, London, Dickens's residence 1851–60 (below)

THE

MUDFOG PAPERS,

ETC.

BY

CHARLES DICKENS,

AUTHOR OF "THE PICKWICK PAPERS," ETC.

NOW FIRST COLLECTED.

LONDON:

RICHARD BENTLEY AND SON,

Publishers in Ordinary to Her Majesty the Queen.

1880.

Title page of the first volume edition of
The Mudfog Papers (1880).

The Mudfog Papers

Introduction

THE PAPERS CONTAINED in this little volume were written by Charles Dickens for the early numbers of *Bentley's Miscellany*.* The manuscripts of the two meetings of the Mudfog Association, and of 'Mr Robert Bolton, the "Gentleman Connected with the Press"', in my possession, are covered with corrections, erasures and additions. At that time Charles Dickens wrote a freer and bolder hand than he came to write in later years, and these manuscripts are easily decipherable.

Something perhaps of the comparative freedom of the hand-writing of these sketches, when set by the side of the manuscript of *Our Mutual Friend*,* may be owing to the quill pen, with whose exit has gone out much of that free and graceful penmanship of which Mr Lupton reminds us that Thomas Tomkins, of St Paul's School, was so unrivalled a teacher.*

GEORGE BENTLEY*

NEW BURLINGTON STREET,

JULY 26TH [1880]

Public Life of Mr Tulrumble,
Once Mayor of Mudfog

MUDFOG IS A PLEASANT TOWN – a remarkably pleasant town – situated in a charming hollow by the side of a river, from which river Mudfog derives an agreeable scent of pitch, tar, coals and rope yarn, a roving population in oilskin hats, a pretty steady influx of drunken bargemen and a great many other maritime advantages. There is a good deal of water about Mudfog, and yet it is not exactly the sort of town for a watering place, either. Water is a perverse sort of element at the best of times, and in Mudfog it is particularly so. In winter, it comes oozing down the streets and tumbling over the fields – nay, rushes into the very cellars and kitchens of the houses, with a lavish prodigality that might well be dispensed with; but in the hot summer weather it *will* dry up and turn green; and, although green is a very good colour in its way, especially in grass, still it certainly is not becoming to water; and it cannot be denied that the beauty of Mudfog is rather impaired, even by this trifling circumstance. Mudfog is a healthy place – very healthy; damp, perhaps, but none the worse for that. It's quite a mistake to suppose that damp is unwholesome: plants thrive best in damp situations, and why shouldn't men? The inhabitants of Mudfog are unanimous in asserting that there exists not a finer race of people on the face of the earth; here we have an indisputable and veracious contradiction of the vulgar error at once. So, admitting Mudfog to be damp, we distinctly state that it is salubrious.

The town of Mudfog is extremely picturesque. Limehouse and Ratcliff Highway* are both something like it, but they give you a very faint idea of Mudfog. There are a great many more public houses in Mudfog – more than in Ratcliff Highway and Limehouse put together. The public buildings, too, are very imposing. We consider the town hall one of the finest specimens of shed architecture extant: it is a combination of the pigsty and tea-garden-box orders; and the simplicity of its design is of surpassing beauty. The idea of placing a large window on one side of the door and a small one on the other is particularly happy. There is a fine bold Doric beauty, too, about the padlock and scraper, which is strictly in keeping with the general effect.

In this room do the Mayor and corporation of Mudfog assemble together in solemn council for the public weal. Seated on the massive wooden benches, which, with the table in the centre, form the only furniture of the whitewashed apartment, the sage men of Mudfog spend hour after hour in grave deliberation. Here they settle at what hour of the night the public houses shall be closed, at what hour of the morning they shall be permitted to open, how soon it shall be lawful for people to eat their dinner on church days and other great political questions; and sometimes, long after silence has fallen on the town and the distant lights from the shops and houses have ceased to twinkle, like far-off stars, to the sight of the boatmen on the river, the illumination in the two unequal-sized windows of the town hall warns the inhabitants of Mudfog that its little body of legislators, like a larger and better-known body of the same genus, a great deal more noisy, and not a whit more profound, are patriotically dozing away in company, far into the night, for their country's good.

Among this knot of sage and learned men, no one was so eminently distinguished, during many years, for the quiet modesty of his appearance and demeanour, as Nicholas Tulrumble, the well-known coal-dealer. However exciting the subject of discussion, however animated the tone of the debate, or however warm the personalities exchanged (and even in Mudfog we get personal sometimes), Nicholas Tulrumble was always the same. To say truth, Nicholas, being an industrious man, and always up betimes, was apt to fall asleep when a debate began, and to remain asleep till it was over, when he would wake up very much refreshed, and give his vote with the greatest complacency. The fact was that Nicholas Tulrumble, knowing that everybody there had made up his mind beforehand, considered the talking as just a long botheration about nothing at all; and to the present hour it remains a question whether, on this point at all events, Nicholas Tulrumble was not pretty near right.

Time, which strews a man's head with silver, sometimes fills his pockets with gold. As he gradually performed one good office for Nicholas Tulrumble, he was obliging enough not to omit the other. Nicholas began life in a wooden tenement of four feet square, with a capital of two and ninepence and a stock-in-trade of three bushels and a half of coals, exclusive of the large lump which hung, by way of signboard, outside. Then he enlarged the shed and kept a truck; then he left the shed, and the truck too, and started a donkey and a Mrs Tulrumble; then he moved again and set up a cart; the cart was soon afterwards exchanged for a wagon; and so he went on like his great predecessor Whittington* – only without a cat for a partner – increasing in wealth and fame, until at last he gave up business altogether, and retired with Mrs Tulrumble and family to Mudfog Hall, which he had himself erected, on something which he attempted to delude himself into the belief was a hill, about a quarter of a mile distant from the town of Mudfog.

About this time, it began to be murmured in Mudfog that Nicholas Tulrumble was growing vain and haughty; that prosperity and success had corrupted the simplicity of his manners and tainted the natural goodness of his heart; in short, that he was setting up for a public character, and a great gentleman, and affected to look down upon his old companions with compassion and contempt. Whether these reports were at the time well founded or not, certain it is that Mrs Tulrumble very shortly afterwards started a four-wheel chaise, driven by a tall postilion in a yellow cap, that Mr Tulrumble junior took to smoking cigars, and calling the footman a "feller", and that Mr Tulrumble from that time forth was no more seen in his old seat in the chimney corner of the Lighterman's Arms at night.

This looked bad; but, more than this, it began to be observed that Mr Nicholas Tulrumble attended the corporation meetings more frequently than heretofore, and he no longer went to sleep as he had done for so many years, but propped his eyelids open with his two forefingers; that he read the newspapers by himself at home; and that he was in the habit of indulging abroad in distant and mysterious allusions to "masses of people", and "the property of the country", and "productive power", and "the monied interest": all of which denoted and proved that Nicholas Tulrumble was either mad or worse; and it puzzled the good people of Mudfog amazingly.

At length, about the middle of the month of October, Mr Tulrumble and family went up to London; the middle of October being, as Mrs Tulrumble informed her acquaintance in Mudfog, the very height of the fashionable season.

Somehow or other, just about this time, despite the health-preserving air of Mudfog, the Mayor died. It was a most extraordinary circumstance; he had lived in Mudfog for eighty-five years. The corporation didn't understand it at all; indeed it was with great difficulty that one old gentleman, who was a great stickler for forms, was dissuaded from proposing a vote of censure on such unaccountable conduct. Strange as it was, however, die he did, without taking the slightest notice of the corporation; and the corporation were imperatively called upon to elect his successor. So, they met for the purpose, and being very full of Nicholas Tulrumble just then, and Nicholas Tulrumble being a very important man, they elected him, and wrote off to London by the very next post to acquaint Nicholas Tulrumble with his new elevation.

Now, it being November time, and Mr Nicholas Tulrumble being in the capital, it fell out that he was present at the Lord Mayor's Show and dinner, at sight of the glory and splendour whereof, he, Mr Tulrumble, was greatly mortified, inasmuch as the reflection would force itself on his mind that, had he been born in London instead of in Mudfog, he might have been a lord mayor too, and have patronized the judges, and been affable to the Lord Chancellor, and friendly with the premier, and coldly condescending to the Secretary to the Treasury, and have dined with a flag behind his back, and done a great many other acts and deeds which unto lord mayors of London peculiarly appertain. The more he thought of the Lord Mayor, the more enviable a personage he seemed. To be a king was all very well; but what was the King to the Lord Mayor! When the King made a speech, everybody knew it was somebody else's writing; whereas here was the Lord Mayor, talking away for half an hour – all out of his own head – amidst the enthusiastic applause of the whole company, while it was notorious that the King might talk to his Parliament till he was black in the face without getting so much as a single cheer. As all these reflections passed through the mind of Mr Nicholas Tulrumble, the Lord Mayor of London appeared to him the greatest sovereign on the face of the earth, beating the Emperor of Russia all to nothing, and leaving the Great Mogul immeasurably behind.

Mr Nicholas Tulrumble was pondering over these things, and inwardly cursing the fate which had pitched his coal shed in Mudfog, when the letter of the corporation was put into his hand. A crimson flush mantled over his face as he read it, for visions of brightness were already dancing before his imagination.

"My dear," said Mr Tulrumble to his wife, "they have elected me mayor of Mudfog."

"Lor-a-mussy!" said Mrs Tulrumble. "Why, what's become of old Sniggs?"

"The late Mr Sniggs, Mrs Tulrumble," said Mr Tulrumble sharply, for he by no means approved of the notion of unceremoniously designating a gentleman who filled the high office of mayor as "Old Sniggs", "the late Mr Sniggs, Mrs Tulrumble, is dead."

The communication was very unexpected; but Mrs Tulrumble only ejaculated "Lor-a-mussy!" once again, as if a mayor were a mere ordinary Christian, at which Mr Tulrumble frowned gloomily.

"What a pity 'tan't in London, ain't it?" said Mrs Tulrumble, after a short pause. "What a pity 'tan't in London, where you might have had a show."

"I *might* have a show in Mudfog, if I thought proper, I apprehend," said Mr Tulrumble mysteriously.

"Lor! So you might, I declare," replied Mrs Tulrumble.

"And a good one too," said Mr Tulrumble.

"Delightful!" exclaimed Mrs Tulrumble.

"One which would rather astonish the ignorant people down there," said Mr Tulrumble.

"It would kill them with envy," said Mrs Tulrumble.

So it was agreed that His Majesty's lieges in Mudfog should be astonished with splendour and slaughtered with envy, and that such a show should take place as had never been seen in that town, or in any other town before – no, not even in London itself.

On the very next day after the receipt of the letter, down came the tall postilion in a post-chaise, not upon one of the horses, but inside – actually inside the chaise – and, driving up to the very door of the town hall, where the corporation were assembled, delivered a letter, written by the Lord knows who, and signed by Nicholas Tulrumble, in which Nicholas said, all through four sides of closely written, gilt-edged, hot-pressed, Bath-post letter paper, that he responded to the call of his fellow townsmen with feelings of heartfelt delight; that he accepted the arduous office which their confidence had imposed upon him; that they would never find him shrinking from the discharge of his duty; that he would endeavour to execute his functions with all that dignity which their magnitude and importance demanded; and a great more to the same effect. But even this was not all. The tall postilion produced from his right-hand top boot a damp copy of that afternoon's number of the county paper; and there, in large type, running the whole length of the very first column, was a long address from Nicholas Tulrumble to the inhabitants of Mudfog, in which he said that he cheerfully complied with their requisition and, in short, as if to prevent any mistake about the matter, told them over again what a grand fellow he meant to be, in very much the same terms as those in which he had already told them all about the matter in his letter.

The corporation stared at one another very hard at all this, and then looked as if for explanation to the tall postilion, but as the tall postilion was intently contemplating the gold tassel on the top of his yellow cap, and could have afforded no explanation whatever, even if his thoughts had been entirely disengaged, they contented themselves with coughing very dubiously and looking very grave. The tall postilion then delivered another letter, in which Nicholas Tulrumble informed the corporation that he intended repairing to the town hall, in grand state and gorgeous procession, on the Monday afternoon next ensuing. At this the corporation looked still more solemn; but, as the epistle wound up with a formal invitation to the whole body to dine with the Mayor on that day, at Mudfog Hall, Mudfog Hill, Mudfog, they began to see the fun of the thing directly, and sent back their compliments, and they'd be sure to come.

Now there happened to be in Mudfog, as somehow or other there does happen to be in almost every town in the British dominions, and perhaps in foreign dominions too – we think it very likely, but, being no great traveller, cannot distinctly say – there happened to be, in Mudfog, a merry-tempered, pleasant-faced, good-for-nothing sort of vagabond, with an invincible dislike to manual labour and an unconquerable attachment to strong beer and spirits, whom everybody knew, and nobody, except his wife, took the trouble to quarrel with, who inherited from his ancestors the appellation of Edward Twigger, and rejoiced in the sobriquet of Bottle-Nosed Ned. He was drunk upon the average once a day, and penitent upon an equally fair calculation once a month; and when he was penitent, he was invariably in the very last stage of maudlin intoxication. He was a ragged, roving, roaring kind of fellow, with a burly form, a sharp wit and a ready head, and could turn his hand to anything when he chose to do it. He was by no means opposed to hard labour on principle, for he would work away at a cricket match by the day together – running, and catching, and batting, and bowling, and revelling in toil which would exhaust a galley slave. He would have been invaluable to a fire office; never was a man with such a natural taste for pumping engines, running up ladders and throwing furniture out of two-pair-of-stairs' windows;* nor was this the only element in which he was at home; he was a humane society in himself, a portable drag, an animated life-preserver, and had saved more people, in his time, from drowning, than the Plymouth lifeboat, or Captain Manby's apparatus.* With all these qualifications, notwithstanding his dissipation, Bottle-Nosed Ned was a general favourite; and the authorities of Mudfog, remembering his numerous services to the population, allowed him in return to get drunk in his own way, without the fear of stocks, fine or imprisonment. He had a general licence, and he showed his sense of the compliment by making the most of it.

We have been thus particular in describing the character and avocations of Bottle-Nosed Ned, because it enables us to introduce a fact politely, without hauling it into the reader's presence with indecent haste by the head and shoulders, and brings us very naturally to relate that on the very same evening on which Mr Nicholas Tulrumble and family returned to Mudfog, Mr Tulrumble's new secretary, just imported from London, with a pale face and light whiskers, thrust his head down to the very bottom of his neckcloth tie, in at the taproom door of the Lighterman's Arms, and enquiring whether one Ned Twigger was luxuriating within, announced himself as the bearer of a message from Nicholas Tulrumble, Esquire, requiring Mr Twigger's immediate attendance at the hall, on private and particular business. It being by no means Mr Twigger's interest to affront the Mayor, he rose from the fireplace with a slight sigh, and followed the light-whiskered secretary through the dirt and wet of Mudfog streets, up to Mudfog Hall, without further ado.

Mr Nicholas Tulrumble was seated in a small cavern with a skylight, which he called his library, sketching out a plan of the procession on a large sheet of paper; and into the cavern the secretary ushered Ned Twigger.

"Well, Twigger!" said Nicholas Tulrumble, condescendingly.

There was a time when Twigger would have replied, "Well, Nick!" but that was in the days of the truck, and a couple of years before the donkey; so he only bowed.

"I want you to go into training, Twigger," said Mr Tulrumble.

"What for, sir?" enquired Ned, with a stare.

"Hush, hush, Twigger!" said the Mayor. "Shut the door, Mr Jennings. Look here, Twigger."

As the Mayor said this, he unlocked a high closet and disclosed a complete suit of brass armour, of gigantic dimensions.

"I want you to wear this next Monday, Twigger," said the Mayor.

"Bless your heart and soul, sir!" replied Ned. "You might as well ask me to wear a seventy-four pounder,* or a cast-iron boiler."

"Nonsense, Twigger, nonsense!" said the Mayor.

"I couldn't stand under it, sir," said Twigger. "It would make mashed potatoes of me, if I attempted it."

"Pooh, pooh, Twigger!" returned the Mayor. "I tell you I have seen it done with my own eyes, in London, and the man wasn't half such a man as you are either."

"I should as soon have thought of a man's wearing the case of an eight-day clock* to save his linen," said Twigger, casting a look of apprehension at the brass suit.

"It's the easiest thing in the world," rejoined the Mayor.

"It's nothing," said Mr Jennings.

"When you're used to it," added Ned.

"You do it by degrees," said the Mayor. "You would begin with one piece tomorrow, and two the next day, and so on, till you had got it all on. Mr Jennings, give Twigger a glass of rum. Just try the breastplate, Twigger. Stay; take another glass of rum first. Help me to lift it, Mr Jennings. Stand firm, Twigger! There! It isn't half as heavy as it looks, is it?"

Twigger was a good strong, stout fellow; so, after a great deal of staggering, he managed to keep himself up, under the breastplate, and even contrived, with the aid of another glass of rum, to walk about in it, and the gauntlets into the bargain. He made a trial of the helmet, but was not equally successful, inasmuch as he tipped over instantly – an accident which Mr Tulrumble clearly demonstrated to be occasioned by his not having a counteracting weight of brass on his legs.

"Now, wear that with grace and propriety on Monday next," said Tulrumble, "and I'll make your fortune."

"I'll try what I can do, sir," said Twigger.

"It must be kept a profound secret," said Tulrumble.

"Of course, sir," replied Twigger.

"And you must be sober," said Tulrumble, "perfectly sober."

Mr Twigger at once solemnly pledged himself to be as sober as a judge, and Nicholas Tulrumble was satisfied, although, had we been Nicholas, we should certainly have exacted some promise of a more specific nature; inasmuch as, having attended the Mudfog assizes in the evening more than once, we can solemnly testify to having seen judges with very strong symptoms of dinner under their wigs. However, that's neither here nor there.

The next day, and the day following, and the day after that, Ned Twigger was securely locked up in the small cavern with the skylight, hard at work at the armour. With every additional piece he could manage to stand upright in, he had an additional glass of rum; and at last, after many partial suffocations, he contrived to get on the whole suit and to stagger up and down the room in it, like an intoxicated effigy from Westminster Abbey.

Never was man so delighted as Nicholas Tulrumble; never was woman so charmed as Nicholas Tulrumble's wife. Here was a sight for the common people of Mudfog! A live man in brass armour! Why, they would go wild with wonder!

The day – *the* Monday – arrived.

If the morning had been made to order, it couldn't have been better adapted to the purpose. They never showed a better fog in London on Lord Mayor's Day than enwrapped the town of Mudfog on that eventful occasion. It had risen slowly and surely from the green and stagnant water with the first light of morning, until it reached a little above the lamp-post tops; and there it had stopped, with a sleepy, sluggish obstinacy, which bade defiance to the sun, who had got up very blood-shot about the eyes, as if he had been at a drinking party over night, and was doing his day's work with the worst possible grace. The thick damp mist hung over the town like a huge gauze curtain. All was dim and dismal. The church steeples had bidden a temporary adieu to the world below, and every object of lesser importance – houses, barns, hedges, trees and barges – had all taken the veil.

The church clock struck one. A cracked trumpet from the front garden of Mudfog Hall produced a feeble flourish, as if some asthmatic person had coughed into it accidentally; the gate flew open, and out came a gentleman, on a moist-sugar-coloured charger, intended to represent a herald, but bearing a much stronger resemblance to a court card* on horseback. This was one of the circus people, who always came down to Mudfog at that time of the year, and who had been engaged by Nicholas Tulrumble expressly for the occasion. There was the horse, whisking his tail about, balancing himself on his hind legs and flourishing away with his forefeet, in a manner which would have gone to the hearts and souls of any reasonable crowd. But a Mudfog crowd never was a reasonable one, and in all probability never will be. Instead of scattering the very fog with their shouts, as they ought most indubitably to have done, and were fully intended to do by Nicholas Tulrumble, they no sooner recognized the herald than they began to growl forth the most unqualified disapprobation at the bare notion of his riding like any other man. If he had come out on his head indeed, or jumping through a hoop, or flying through a red-hot drum, or even standing on one leg with his other foot in his mouth, they might have had something to say to him; but for a professional gentleman to sit astride in the saddle, with his feet in the stirrups, was rather too good a joke. So, the herald was a decided failure, and the crowd hooted with great energy, as he pranced ingloriously away.

On the procession came. We are afraid to say how many supernumeraries there were, in striped shirts and black velvet caps, to imitate the London watermen, or how many base imitations of running footmen, or how many banners, which, owing to the heaviness of the atmosphere, could by no means be prevailed on to display their inscriptions; still less do we feel disposed to relate how the men who played the wind instruments, looking up into the sky (we mean the fog) with musical fervour, walked through pools of water and hillocks of mud, till they covered the powdered heads of the running footmen aforesaid with splashes that looked curious, but not ornamental; or how the barrel-organ performer put on the wrong stop and played one tune while the band played another; or how the horses, being used to the arena, and not to the streets, would stand still and dance, instead of going on and prancing – all of which are matters which might be dilated upon to great advantage, but which we have not the least intention of dilating upon, notwithstanding.

Oh! It was a grand and beautiful sight to behold a corporation in glass coaches, provided at the sole cost and charge of Nicholas Tulrumble, coming rolling along, like a funeral out of mourning, and to watch the attempts the corporation made to look great and solemn, when Nicholas Tulrumble himself, in the four-wheel chaise, with the tall postilion, rolled out after them, with Mr Jennings on one side to look like a chaplain and a supernumerary on the other, with an old Life Guardsman's sabre,* to imitate the sword-bearer; and to see the tears rolling down the faces of the mob as they screamed with merriment. This was beautiful! And so was the appearance of Mrs Tulrumble and son, as they bowed with grave dignity out of their coach window to all the dirty faces that were laughing around them – but it is not even with this that we have to do, but with the sudden stopping of the procession at another blast of the trumpet, whereat, and whereupon, a profound silence ensued, and all eyes were turned towards Mudfog Hall, in the confident anticipation of some new wonder.

"They won't laugh now, Mr Jennings," said Nicholas Tulrumble.

"I think not, sir," said Mr Jennings.

"See how eager they look," said Nicholas Tulrumble. "Aha! The laugh will be on our side now, eh, Mr Jennings?"

"No doubt of that, sir," replied Mr Jennings; and Nicholas Tulrumble, in a state of pleasurable excitement, stood up in the four-wheel chaise and telegraphed gratification to the Mayoress behind.

While all this was going forward, Ned Twigger had descended into the kitchen of Mudfog Hall for the purpose of indulging the servants with a private view of the curiosity that was to burst upon the town; and, somehow or other, the footman was so companionable, and the housemaid so kind, and the cook so friendly, that he could not resist the offer of the first-mentioned to sit down and take something – just to drink success to master in.

So, down Ned Twigger sat himself in his brass livery on the top of the kitchen table, and in a mug of something strong, paid for by the unconscious Nicholas Tulrumble, and provided by the companionable footman, drank success to the Mayor and his procession; and, as Ned laid by his helmet to imbibe the something strong, the companionable footman put it on his own head, to the immeasurable and unrecordable delight of the cook and housemaid. The companionable footman was very facetious to Ned, and Ned was very gallant to the cook and housemaid by turns. They were all very cosy and comfortable, and the something strong went briskly round.

At last Ned Twigger was loudly called for by the procession people; and, having had his helmet fixed on, in a very complicated manner, by the companionable footman and the kind housemaid and the friendly cook, he walked gravely forth, and appeared before the multitude.

The crowd roared – it was not with wonder, it was not with surprise: it was most decidedly and unquestionably with laughter.

"What!" said Mr Tulrumble, starting up in the four-wheel chaise. "Laughing? If they laugh at a man in real brass armour, they'd laugh when their own fathers were dying. Why doesn't he go into his place, Mr Jennings? What's he rolling down towards us for? He has no business here!"

"I am afraid, sir…" faltered Mr Jennings.

"Afraid of what, sir?" said Nicholas Tulrumble, looking up into the secretary's face.

"I am afraid he's drunk, sir," replied Mr Jennings.

Nicholas Tulrumble took one look at the extraordinary figure that was bearing down upon them, and then, clasping his secretary by the arm, uttered an audible groan in anguish of spirit.

It is a melancholy fact that Mr Twigger, having full licence to demand a single glass of rum on the putting on of every piece of the armour, got, by some means or other, rather out of his calculation in the hurry and confusion of preparation, and drank about four glasses to a piece instead of one, not to mention the something strong which went on the top of it. Whether the brass armour checked the natural flow of perspiration and thus prevented the spirit from evaporating, we are not scientific enough to know; but, whatever the cause was, Mr Twigger no sooner found himself outside the gate of Mudfog Hall than he also found himself in a very considerable state of intoxication – and hence his extraordinary style of progressing. This was bad enough, but, as if fate and fortune had conspired against Nicholas Tulrumble, Mr Twigger, not having been penitent for a good calendar month, took it into his head to be most especially and particularly sentimental, just when his repentance could have been most conveniently dispensed with. Immense tears were rolling down his cheeks, and he was vainly endeavouring to conceal his grief by applying to his eyes a blue cotton pocket handkerchief with white spots – an article not strictly in keeping with a suit of armour some three hundred years old or thereabouts.

"Twigger, you villain!" said Nicholas Tulrumble, quite forgetting his dignity, "go back."

"Never," said Ned. "I'm a miserable wretch. I'll never leave you."

The bystanders of course received this declaration with acclamations of "That's right, Ned, don't!"

"I don't intend it," said Ned, with all the obstinacy of a very tipsy man. "I'm very unhappy. I'm the wretched father of an unfortunate family, but I am very faithful, sir. I'll never leave you." Having reiterated this obliging promise, Ned proceeded in broken words to harangue the crowd upon the number of years he had lived in Mudfog, the excessive respectability of his character and other topics of the like nature.

"Here! Will anybody lead him away?" said Nicholas. "If they'll call on me afterwards, I'll reward them well."

Two or three men stepped forward, with the view of bearing Ned off, when the secretary interposed.

"Take care! Take care!" said Mr Jennings. "I beg your pardon, sir, but they'd better not go too near him, because if he falls over, he'll certainly crush somebody."

At this hint the crowd retired on all sides to a very respectful distance, and left Ned, like the Duke of Devonshire, in a little circle of his own.

"But, Mr Jennings," said Nicholas Tulrumble, "he'll be suffocated."

"I'm very sorry for it, sir," replied Mr Jennings, "but nobody can get that armour off without his own assistance. I'm quite certain of it from the way he put it on."

Here Ned wept dolefully, and shook his helmeted head, in a manner that might have touched a heart of stone; but the crowd had not hearts of stone, and they laughed heartily.

"Dear me, Mr Jennings," said Nicholas, turning pale at the possibility of Ned's being smothered in his antique costume. "Dear me, Mr Jennings, can nothing be done with him?"

"Nothing at all," replied Ned, "nothing at all. Gentlemen, I'm an unhappy wretch. I'm a body, gentlemen, in a brass coffin." At this poetical idea of his own conjuring up, Ned cried so much that the people began to get sympathetic, and to ask what Nicholas Tulrumble meant by putting a man into such a machine as that; and one individual in a hairy waistcoat like the top of a trunk, who had previously expressed his opinion that if Ned hadn't been a poor man, Nicholas wouldn't have dared do it, hinted at the propriety of breaking the four-wheel chaise, or Nicholas's head, or both, which last compound proposition the crowd seemed to consider a very good notion.

It was not acted upon, however, for it had hardly been broached when Ned Twigger's wife made her appearance abruptly in the little circle before noticed, and Ned no sooner caught a glimpse of her face and form than from the mere force of habit he set off towards his home just as fast as his legs could carry him; and that was not very quick in the present instance either, for however ready they might have been to carry *him*, they couldn't get on very well under the brass armour. So Mrs Twigger had plenty of time to denounce Nicholas Tulrumble to his face; to express her opinion that he was a decided monster; and to intimate that, if her ill-used husband sustained any personal damage from the brass armour, she would have the law of Nicholas Tulrumble for manslaughter. When she had said all this with due vehemence, she posted after Ned, who was dragging himself along as best he could, and deploring his unhappiness in most dismal tones.

What a wailing and screaming Ned's children raised when he got home at last! Mrs Twigger tried to undo the armour, first in one place and then in another, but she couldn't manage it; so she tumbled Ned into bed, helmet, armour, gauntlets and all. Such a creaking as the bedstead made, under Ned's weight in his new suit! It didn't break down though, and there Ned lay, like the anonymous vessel in the Bay of Biscay, till next day,* drinking barley water, and looking miserable – and every time he groaned, his good lady said it served him right, which was all the consolation Ned Twigger got.

Nicholas Tulrumble and the gorgeous procession went on together to the town hall, amid the hisses and groans of all the spectators, who had suddenly taken it into their heads to consider poor Ned a martyr. Nicholas was formally installed in his new office, in acknowledgement of which ceremony he delivered himself of a speech, composed by the secretary, which was very long, and no doubt very good, only the noise of the people outside prevented anybody from hearing it but Nicholas Tulrumble himself. After which, the procession got back to Mudfog Hall any how it could, and Nicholas and the corporation sat down to dinner.

But the dinner was flat, and Nicholas was disappointed. They were such dull sleepy old fellows, that corporation. Nicholas made quite as long speeches as the Lord Mayor of London had done, nay, he said the very same things that the Lord Mayor of

London had said, and the deuce a cheer the corporation gave him. There was only one man in the party who was thoroughly awake, and he was insolent and called him Nick. Nick! What would be the consequence, thought Nicholas, of anybody presuming to call the Lord Mayor of London "Nick"! He should like to know what the sword-bearer would say to that; or the recorder, or the toastmaster, or any other of the great officers of the city. They'd nick him.

But these were not the worst of Nicholas Tulrumble's doings. If they had been, he might have remained a mayor to this day and have talked till he lost his voice. He contracted a relish for statistics and got philosophical, and the statistics and the philosophy together led him into an act which increased his unpopularity and hastened his downfall.

At the very end of the Mudfog high street, and abutting on the riverside, stands the Jolly Boatmen, an old-fashioned low-roofed, bay-windowed house, with a bar, kitchen and taproom all in one, and a large fireplace with a kettle to correspond, round which the working men have congregated time out of mind on a winter's night, refreshed by draughts of good strong beer and cheered by the sounds of a fiddle and tambourine – the Jolly Boatmen having been duly licensed by the Mayor and corporation, to scrape the fiddle and thumb the tambourine from time, whereof the memory of the oldest inhabitants goeth not to the contrary. Now Nicholas Tulrumble had been reading pamphlets on crime, and parliamentary reports – or had made the secretary read them to him, which is the same thing in effect – and he at once perceived that this fiddle and tambourine must have done more to demoralize Mudfog than any other operating causes that ingenuity could imagine. So he read up for the subject, and determined to come out on the corporation with a burst, the very next time the licence was applied for.

The licensing day came, and the red-faced landlord of the Jolly Boatmen walked into the town hall, looking as jolly as need be, having actually put on an extra fiddle for that night, to commemorate the anniversary of the Jolly Boatmen's music licence. It was applied for in due form, and was just about to be granted as a matter of course, when up rose Nicholas Tulrumble and drowned the astonished corporation in a torrent of eloquence. He descanted in glowing terms upon the increasing depravity of his native town of Mudfog, and the excesses committed by its population. Then he related how shocked he had been to see barrels of beer sliding down into the cellar of the Jolly Boatmen week after week; and how he had sat at a window opposite the Jolly Boatmen for two days together, to count the people who went in for beer between the hours of twelve and one o'clock alone – which, by the by, was the time at which the great majority of the Mudfog people dined. Then he went on to state how the number of people who came out with beer jugs averaged twenty-one in five minutes, which, being multiplied by twelve, gave two hundred and fifty-two people with beer jugs in an hour, and multiplied again by fifteen (the number of hours during which the house was open daily) yielded three thousand, seven hundred and eighty people with beer jugs per day, or twenty-six thousand, four hundred and sixty people with beer jugs per week. Then he proceeded to show that a tambourine and moral degradation were synonymous terms, and a fiddle and vicious propensities wholly inseparable. All these arguments he strengthened and demonstrated by frequent references to a large book with a blue cover, and sundry quotations from the Middlesex magistrates; and in the end, the corporation, who were posed with the figures and sleepy with the speech, and sadly in want of dinner into the bargain, yielded the palm to Nicholas Tulrumble and refused the music licence to the Jolly Boatmen.

But although Nicholas triumphed, his triumph was short. He carried on the war against beer jugs and fiddles, forgetting the time when he was glad to drink out of the one and to dance to the other, till the people hated and his old friends shunned him. He grew tired of the lonely magnificence of Mudfog Hall, and his heart yearned towards the Lighterman's Arms. He wished he had never set up as a public man, and sighed for the good old times of the coal shop and the chimney corner.

At length old Nicholas, being thoroughly miserable, took heart of grace, paid the secretary a quarter's wages in advance and packed him off to London by the next coach. Having taken this step, he put his hat on his head, and his pride in his pocket, and walked down to the old room at the Lighterman's Arms. There were only two of the old fellows there, and they looked coldly on Nicholas as he proffered his hand.

"Are you going to put down pipes, Mr Tulrumble?" said one.

"Or trace the progress of crime to 'bacca?" growled another.

"Neither," replied Nicholas Tulrumble, shaking hands with them both, whether they would or not. "I've come down to say that I'm very sorry for having made a fool of myself, and that I hope you'll give me up the old chair again."

The old fellows opened their eyes, and three or four more old fellows opened the door, to whom Nicholas, with tears in his eyes, thrust out his hand too, and told the same story. They raised a shout of joy that made the bells in the ancient church tower vibrate again, and wheeling the old chair into the warm corner, thrust old Nicholas down into it and ordered in the very largest-sized bowl of hot punch, with an unlimited number of pipes, directly.

The next day, the Jolly Boatmen got the licence, and the next night, old Nicholas and Ned Twigger's wife led off a dance to the music of the fiddle and tambourine, the tone of which seemed mightily improved by a little rest, for they never had played so merrily before. Ned Twigger was in the very height of his glory, and he danced hornpipes, and balanced chairs on his chin, and straws on his nose, till the whole company, including the corporation, were in raptures of admiration at the brilliancy of his acquirements.

Mr Tulrumble, Junior, couldn't make up his mind to be anything but magnificent, so he went up to London and drew bills on his father; and when he had overdrawn and got into debt, he grew penitent, and came home again.

As to old Nicholas, he kept his word, and having had six weeks of public life, never tried it any more. He went to sleep in the town hall at the very next meeting, and, in full proof of his sincerity, has requested us to write this faithful narrative. We wish it could have the effect of reminding the Tulrumbles of another sphere that puffed-up conceit is not dignity, and that snarling at the little pleasures they were once glad to enjoy, because they would rather forget the times when they were of lower station, renders them objects of contempt and ridicule.

This is the first time we have published any of our gleanings from this particular source. Perhaps, at some future period, we may venture to open the chronicles of Mudfog.

Full Report of the First Meeting
of the Mudfog Association for the
Advancement of Everything

W E HAVE MADE the most unparalleled *and extraordinary exertions to place before our readers a complete
and accurate account of the proceedings at the late grand
meeting of the Mudfog Association, holden in the town of
Mudfog; it affords us great happiness to lay the result before
them, in the shape of various communications received from
our able, talented and graphic correspondent, expressly sent
down for the purpose, who has immortalized us, himself,
Mudfog and the association, all at one and the same time.
We have been, indeed, for some days unable to determine who
will transmit the greatest name to posterity: ourselves, who
sent our correspondent down; our correspondent, who wrote
an account of the matter; or the association, who gave our
correspondent something to write about. We rather incline
to the opinion that we are the greatest man of the party,
inasmuch as the notion of an exclusive and authentic report
originated with us; this may be prejudice: it may arise from
a prepossession on our part in our own favour. Be it so. We
have no doubt that every gentleman concerned in this mighty
assemblage is troubled with the same complaint in a greater

or less degree, and it is a consolation to us to know that we have at least this feeling in common with the great scientific stars, the brilliant and extraordinary luminaries, whose speculations we record.

We give our correspondent's letters in the order in which they reached us. Any attempt at amalgamating them into one beautiful whole would only destroy that glowing tone, that dash of wildness and rich vein of picturesque interest, which pervade them throughout.

"*Mudfog, Monday night, seven o'clock.*
"We are in a state of great excitement here. Nothing is spoken of but the approaching meeting of the association. The inn doors are thronged with waiters anxiously looking for the expected arrivals, and the numerous bills which are wafered up in the windows of private houses, intimating that there are beds to let within, give the streets a very animated and cheerful appearance, the wafers being of a great variety of colours, and the monotony of printed inscriptions being relieved by every possible size and style of handwriting. It is confidently rumoured that Professors Snore, Doze and Wheezy have engaged three beds and a sitting room at the Pig and Tinderbox. I give you the rumour as it has reached me; but I cannot, as yet, vouch for its accuracy. The moment I have been enabled to obtain any certain information upon this interesting point, you may depend upon receiving it."

"*Half-past seven.*

"I have just returned from a personal interview with the landlord of the Pig and Tinderbox. He speaks confidently of the probability of Professors Snore, Doze and Wheezy taking up their residence at his house during the sitting of the association, but denies that the beds have been yet engaged; in which representation he is confirmed by the chambermaid – a girl of artless manners and interesting appearance. The boots denies that it is at all likely that Professors Snore, Doze and Wheezy will put up here, but I have reason to believe that this man has been suborned by the proprietor of the Original Pig, which is the opposition hotel. Amidst such conflicting testimony it is difficult to arrive at the real truth; but you may depend upon receiving authentic information upon this point the moment the fact is ascertained. The excitement still continues. A boy fell through the window of the pastry cook's shop at the corner of the high street about half an hour ago, which has occasioned much confusion. The general impression is that it was an accident. Pray Heaven it may prove so!"

"*Tuesday, noon.*

"At an early hour this morning the bells of all the churches struck seven o'clock; the effect of which, in the present lively state of the town, was extremely singular. While I was at breakfast, a yellow gig, drawn by a dark-grey horse with a patch of white over his right eyelid, proceeded at a rapid pace in the direction of the Original Pig stables; it is currently reported that this gentleman has arrived here for the purpose of attending the association, and from what I have heard, I consider it extremely probable, although nothing decisive is yet known regarding him. You may conceive the anxiety with which we are all looking forward to the arrival of the four-o'clock coach this afternoon.

"Notwithstanding the excited state of the populace, no outrage has yet been committed, owing to the admirable discipline and discretion of the police, who are nowhere to be seen. A barrel organ is playing opposite my window, and groups of people, offering fish and vegetables for sale, parade the streets. With these exceptions everything is quiet, and I trust will continue so."

"*Five o'clock*.

"It is now ascertained, beyond all doubt, that Professors Snore, Doze and Wheezy will *not* repair to the Pig and Tinderbox, but have actually engaged apartments at the Original Pig. This intelligence is *exclusive*, and I leave you and your readers to draw their own inferences from it. Why Professor Wheezy, of all people in the world, should repair to the Original Pig in preference to the Pig and Tinderbox, it is not easy to conceive. The Professor is a man who should be above all such petty feelings. Some people here openly impute treachery, and a distinct breach of faith to Professors Snore and Doze; while others, again, are disposed to acquit them of any culpability in the transaction, and to insinuate that the blame rests solely with Professor Wheezy. I own that I incline to the latter opinion, and although it gives me great pain to speak in terms of censure or disapprobation of a man of such transcendent genius and acquirements, still I am bound to say that, if my suspicions be well founded, and if all the reports which have reached my ears be true, I really do not well know what to make of the matter.

"Mr Slug, so celebrated for his statistical researches, arrived this afternoon by the four-o'clock stage. His complexion is a dark purple, and he has a habit of sighing constantly. He looked extremely well, and appeared in high health and spirits. Mr Woodensconce also came down in the same conveyance. The distinguished gentleman was fast asleep on his arrival, and I am informed by the guard that he had been so the whole way. He was, no doubt, preparing for his approaching fatigues; but what gigantic visions must those be that flit through the brain of such a man when his body is in a state of torpidity!

"The influx of visitors increases every moment. I am told (I know not how truly) that two post-chaises have arrived at the Original Pig within the last half-hour, and I myself observed a wheelbarrow, containing three carpetbags and a bundle, entering the yard of the Pig and Tinderbox no longer ago than five minutes since. The people are still quietly pursuing their ordinary occupations, but there is a wildness in their eyes, and an unwonted rigidity in the muscles of their countenances, which shows to the observant spectator that their expectations are strained to the very utmost pitch. I fear, unless some very extraordinary arrivals take place tonight, that consequences may arise from this popular ferment which every man of sense and feeling would deplore."

"*Twenty minutes past six*.
"I have just heard that the boy who fell through the pastry cook's window last night has died of the fright. He was suddenly called upon to pay three and sixpence for the damage done, and his constitution, it seems, was not strong enough to bear up against the shock. The inquest, it is said, will be held tomorrow."

"*Three quarters past seven*.
"Professors Muff and Nogo have just driven up to the hotel door; they at once ordered dinner with great condescension. We are all very much delighted with the urbanity of their manners, and the ease with which they adapt themselves to the forms and ceremonies of ordinary life. Immediately on their arrival they sent for the head waiter, and privately requested him to purchase a live dog – as cheap a one as he could meet with – and to send him up after dinner, with a pie board, a knife and fork and a clean plate. It is conjectured that some experiments will be tried upon the dog tonight; if any particulars should transpire, I will forward them by express."

"*Half-past eight*.
"The animal has been procured. He is a pug dog, of rather intelligent appearance, in good condition, and with very short

legs. He has been tied to a curtain peg in a dark room, and is howling dreadfully."

"*Ten minutes to nine.*
"The dog has just been rung for. With an instinct which would appear almost the result of reason, the sagacious animal seized the waiter by the calf of the leg when he approached to take him, and made a desperate, though ineffectual resistance. I have not been able to procure admission to the apartment occupied by the scientific gentlemen; but, judging from the sounds which reached my ears when I stood upon the landing place outside the door, just now, I should be disposed to say that the dog had retreated growling beneath some article of furniture, and was keeping the professors at bay. This conjecture is confirmed by the testimony of the ostler, who, after peeping through the keyhole, assures me that he distinctly saw Professor Nogo on his knees, holding forth a small bottle of prussic acid, to which the animal, who was crouched beneath an armchair, obstinately declined to smell. You cannot imagine the feverish state of irritation we are in, lest the interests of science should be sacrificed to the prejudices of a brute creature who is not endowed with sufficient sense to foresee the incalculable benefits which the whole human race may derive from so very slight a concession on his part."

"*Nine o'clock.*
"The dog's tail and ears have been sent downstairs to be washed; from which circumstance we infer that the animal is

no more. His forelegs have been delivered to the boots to be brushed, which strengthens the supposition."

"Half after ten.

"My feelings are so overpowered by what has taken place in the course of the last hour and a half that I have scarcely strength to detail the rapid succession of events which have quite bewildered all those who are cognizant of their occurrence. It appears that the pug dog mentioned in my last was surreptitiously obtained – stolen, in fact – by some person attached to the stable department, from an unmarried lady resident in this town. Frantic on discovering the loss of her favourite, the lady rushed distractedly into the street, calling in the most heart-rending and pathetic manner upon the passengers to restore her, her Augustus – for so the deceased was named, in affectionate remembrance of a former lover of his mistress, to whom he bore a striking personal resemblance, which renders the circumstances additionally affecting. I am not yet in a condition to inform you what circumstance induced the bereaved lady to direct her steps to the hotel which had witnessed the last struggles of her protégé. I can only state that she arrived there, at the very instant when his detached members were passing through the passage on a small tray. Her shrieks still reverberate in my ears! I grieve to say that the expressive features of Professor Muff were much scratched and lacerated by the injured lady; and that Professor Nogo, besides sustaining several severe bites, has lost some handfuls of hair from the same cause. It must be some consolation to these gentlemen to know that their ardent attachment to scientific pursuits has alone occasioned these unpleasant consequences, for which the sympathy of a grateful country will sufficiently reward them. The unfortunate lady remains at the Pig and Tinderbox, and up to this time is reported in a very precarious state.

"I need scarcely tell you that this unlooked-for catastrophe has cast a damp and gloom upon us in the midst of our exhilaration; natural in any case, but greatly enhanced in this, by the amiable qualities of the deceased animal, who appears to have been much and deservedly respected by the whole of his acquaintance."

"*Twelve o'clock.*

"I take the last opportunity before sealing my parcel to inform you that the boy who fell through the pastry cook's window is not dead, as was universally believed, but alive and well. The report appears to have had its origin in his mysterious disappearance. He was found half an hour since on the premises of a sweet-stuff maker, where a raffle had been announced for a second-hand sealskin cap and a tambourine; and where – a sufficient number of members not having been obtained at first – he had patiently waited until the list was completed. This fortunate discovery has in some degree restored our gaiety and cheerfulness. It is proposed to get up a subscription for him without delay.

"Everybody is nervously anxious to see what tomorrow will bring forth. If anyone should arrive in the course of the night,

I have left strict directions to be called immediately. I should have sat up, indeed, but the agitating events of this day have been too much for me.

"No news yet of either of the Professors Snore, Doze or Wheezy. It is very strange!"

"*Wednesday afternoon.*

"All is now over; and, upon one point at least, I am at length enabled to set the minds of your readers at rest. The three professors arrived at ten minutes after two o'clock, and, instead of taking up their quarters at the Original Pig, as it was universally understood in the course of yesterday that they would assuredly have done, drove straight to the Pig and Tinderbox, where they threw off the mask at once, and openly announced their intention of remaining. Professor Wheezy *may* reconcile this very extraordinary conduct with *his* notions of fair and equitable dealing, but I would recommend Professor Wheezy to be cautious how he presumes too far upon his well-earned reputation. How such a man as Professor Snore, or, which is still more extraordinary, such an individual as Professor Doze, can quietly allow himself to be mixed up with such proceedings as these, you will naturally enquire. Upon this head, rumour is silent; I have my speculations, but forbear to give utterance to them just now."

"*Four o'clock.*

"The town is filling fast; eighteenpence has been offered for a bed and refused. Several gentlemen were under the necessity last night of sleeping in the brickfields, and on the steps of doors, for which they were taken before the magistrates in a body this morning, and committed to prison as vagrants for various terms. One of these persons I understand to be a highly respectable tinker, of great practical skill, who had forwarded a paper to the president of Section D – Mechanical Science, on the construction of pipkins with copper bottoms and safety valves, of which report speaks highly. The incarceration of this gentleman is greatly to be regretted, as his absence will preclude any discussion on the subject.

"The bills are being taken down in all directions, and lodgings are being secured on almost any terms. I have heard of fifteen shillings a week for two rooms, exclusive of coals and attendance, but I can scarcely believe it. The excitement is dreadful. I was informed this morning that the civil authorities, apprehensive of some outbreak of popular feeling, had commanded a recruiting sergeant and two corporals to be under arms; and that, with the view of not irritating the people unnecessarily by their presence, they had been requested to take up their position before daybreak in a turnpike, distant about a quarter of a mile from the town. The vigour and promptness of these measures cannot be too highly extolled.

"Intelligence has just been brought me that an elderly female, in a state of inebriety, has declared in the open street her intention to 'do' for Mr Slug. Some statistical returns compiled by that gentleman, relative to the consumption of raw spirituous liquors in this place, are supposed to be the cause of the wretch's animosity. It is added that this declaration was loudly cheered by a crowd of persons who had assembled on the spot; and that one man had the boldness to designate Mr Slug aloud by the opprobrious epithet of 'Stick-in-the-mud'! It is earnestly to be hoped that now, when the moment has arrived for their interference, the magistrates will not shrink from the exercise of that power which is vested in them by the constitution of our common country."

"*Half-past ten*.

"The disturbance, I am happy to inform you, has been completely quelled, and the ringleader taken into custody. She had a pail of cold water thrown over her, previous to being locked up, and expresses great contrition and uneasiness. We are all in a fever of anticipation about tomorrow; but, now that we are within a few hours of the meeting of the association, and at last enjoy the proud consciousness of having its illustrious members amongst us, I trust and hope everything may go off peaceably. I shall send you a full report of tomorrow's proceedings by the night coach."

"*Eleven o'clock*.

"I open my letter to say that nothing whatever has occurred since I folded it up."

"*Thursday*.

"The sun rose this morning at the usual hour. I did not observe anything particular in the aspect of the glorious planet, except that he appeared to me (it might have been a delusion of my heightened fancy) to shine with more than common brilliancy, and to shed a refulgent lustre upon the town, such as I had never observed before. This is the more extraordinary as the sky was perfectly cloudless, and the atmosphere peculiarly fine. At half-past nine o'clock the general committee assembled, with the last year's president in the chair. The report of the council was read, and one passage, which stated that the council had corresponded with no less than three thousand, five hundred and seventy-one persons (all of whom paid their own postage), on no fewer than seven thousand, two hundred and forty-three topics, was received with a degree of enthusiasm which no efforts could suppress. The various committees and sections having been appointed, and the more formal business transacted, the great proceedings of the meeting commenced at eleven o'clock precisely. I had the happiness of occupying a most eligible position at that time, in

"Section A – Zoology and Botany
Great room, Pig and Tinderbox.
President – Professor Snore. Vice Presidents – Professors
Doze and Wheezy.

"The scene at this moment was particularly striking. The sun streamed through the windows of the apartments, and tinted the whole scene with its brilliant rays, bringing out in strong relief the noble visages of the professors and scientific gentlemen who, some with bald heads, some with red heads, some with brown heads, some with grey heads, some with black heads, some with block heads, presented a *coup d'œil* which no eyewitness will readily forget. In front of these gentlemen were papers and inkstands; and round the room, on elevated benches extending as far as the forms could reach, were assembled a brilliant concourse of those lovely and elegant women for which Mudfog is justly acknowledged to be without a rival in the whole world. The contrast between their fair faces and the dark coats and trousers of the scientific gentlemen I shall never cease to remember while Memory holds her seat.

"Time having been allowed for a slight confusion, occasioned by the falling-down of the greater part of the platforms, to subside, the President called on one of the secretaries to read a communication entitled 'Some remarks on the industrious fleas, with considerations on the importance of establishing infant schools among that numerous class of society; of directing their industry to useful and practical ends; and of applying the surplus fruits thereof, towards providing for them a comfortable and respectable maintenance in their old age'.

"THE AUTHOR stated that, having long turned his attention to the moral and social condition of these interesting animals, he had been induced to visit an exhibition in Regent Street, London, commonly known by the designation of 'The Industrious Fleas'.* He had there seen many fleas, occupied certainly in various pursuits and avocations, but occupied, he was bound to add, in a manner which no man of well-regulated mind could fail to regard with sorrow and regret. One flea, reduced to the level of a beast of burden, was drawing about a miniature gig, containing a particularly small effigy of His Grace the Duke of Wellington; while another was staggering beneath the weight of a golden model of his great adversary Napoleon Bonaparte. Some, brought up as mountebanks and ballet dancers, were performing a figure dance (he regretted to observe that, of the fleas so employed, several were females); others were in training, in a small cardboard box, for pedestrians – mere sporting characters – and two were actually engaged in the cold-blooded and barbarous occupation of duelling; a pursuit from which humanity recoiled with horror and disgust. He suggested that measures should be immediately taken to employ the labour of these fleas as part and parcel of the productive power of the country, which might easily be done by the establishment among them of infant schools and houses of industry, in which a system of virtuous education, based upon sound principles, should be observed, and moral precepts strictly inculcated. He proposed that every flea who presumed to exhibit, for hire, music or dancing, or any species of theatrical entertainment, without a licence, should be considered a vagabond, and treated accordingly; in which respect he only placed him upon a level with the rest of mankind. He would further suggest that their labour should be placed under the control and regulation of the state, who should set apart from the profits a fund for the support of superannuated or disabled fleas, their widows and orphans. With this view, he proposed that liberal premiums should be offered for the three

46

best designs for a general almshouse; from which – as insect architecture was well known to be in a very advanced and perfect state – we might possibly derive many valuable hints for the improvement of our metropolitan universities, national galleries and other public edifices.

"THE PRESIDENT wished to be informed how the ingenious gentleman proposed to open a communication with fleas generally, in the first instance, so that they might be thoroughly imbued with a sense of the advantages they must necessarily derive from changing their mode of life and applying themselves to honest labour. This appeared to him the only difficulty.

"THE AUTHOR submitted that this difficulty was easily overcome, or rather that there was no difficulty at all in the case. Obviously the course to be pursued, if Her Majesty's Government could be prevailed upon to take up the plan, would be to secure at a remunerative salary the individual to whom he had alluded as presiding over the exhibition in Regent Street at the period of his visit. That gentleman would at once be able to put himself in communication with the mass of the fleas, and to instruct them in pursuance of some general plan of education, to be sanctioned by Parliament, until such time as the more intelligent among them were advanced enough to officiate as teachers to the rest.

"THE PRESIDENT and several members of the section highly complimented the author of the paper last read, on his most ingenious and important treatise. It was determined that the subject should be recommended to the immediate consideration of the council.

"Mr Wigsby produced a cauliflower somewhat larger than a chaise umbrella, which had been raised by no other artificial means than the simple application of highly carbonated soda water as manure. He explained that by scooping out the head, which would afford a new and delicious species of nourishment for the poor, a parachute, in principle something similar to that constructed by M. Garnerin,* was at once obtained; the stalk of course being kept downwards. He added that he was perfectly willing to make a descent from a height of not less than three miles and a quarter, and had in fact already proposed the same to the proprietors of Vauxhall Gardens,* who in the handsomest manner at once consented to his wishes and appointed an early day next summer for the undertaking; merely stipulating that the rim of the cauliflower should be previously broken in three or four places to ensure the safety of the descent.

"The President congratulated the public on the grand gala in store for them, and warmly eulogized the proprietors of the establishment alluded to, for their love of science and regard for the safety of human life, both of which did them the highest honour.

"A member wished to know how many thousand additional lamps the royal property would be illuminated with, on the night after the descent.

"Mr Wigsby replied that the point was not yet finally decided; but he believed it was proposed, over and above the ordinary illuminations, to exhibit in various devices eight millions and a half of additional lamps.

"THE MEMBER expressed himself much gratified with this announcement.

"MR BLUNDERBUM delighted the section with a most interesting and valuable paper 'on the last moments of the learned pig', which produced a very strong impression on the assembly, the account being compiled from the personal recollections of his favourite attendant. The account stated in the most emphatic terms that the animal's name was not Toby, but Solomon; and distinctly proved that he could have no near relatives in the profession, as many designing persons had falsely stated, inasmuch as his father, mother, brothers and sisters had all fallen victims to the butcher at different times. An uncle of his indeed had with very great labour been traced to a sty in Somers Town;* but as he was in a very infirm state at the time, being afflicted with measles, and shortly afterwards disappeared, there appeared too much reason to conjecture that he had been converted into sausages. The disorder of the learned pig was originally a severe cold, which, being aggravated by excessive trough indulgence, finally settled upon the lungs, and terminated in a general decay of the constitution. A melancholy instance of a presentiment entertained by the animal of his approaching dissolution was recorded. After gratifying a numerous and fashionable company with his performances, in which no falling-off whatever was visible, he fixed his eyes on the biographer and, turning to the watch which lay on the floor, and on which he was accustomed to point out the hour, deliberately passed his snout twice round the dial. In precisely four-and-twenty hours from that time he had ceased to exist!

"Professor Wheezy enquired whether, previous to his demise, the animal had expressed, by signs or otherwise, any wishes regarding the disposal of his little property.

"Mr Blunderbum replied that when the biographer took up the pack of cards at the conclusion of the performance, the animal grunted several times in a significant manner, and nodding his head as he was accustomed to do when gratified. From these gestures it was understood that he wished the attendant to keep the cards, which he had ever since done. He had not expressed any wish relative to his watch, which had accordingly been pawned by the same individual.

"The President wished to know whether any member of the section had ever seen or conversed with the pig-faced lady, who was reported to have worn a black velvet mask, and to have taken her meals from a golden trough.

"After some hesitation a member replied that the pig-faced lady was his mother-in-law, and that he trusted the President would not violate the sanctity of private life.

"The President begged pardon. He had considered the pig-faced lady a public character. Would the honourable member object to state, with a view to the advancement of science, whether she was in any way connected with the learned pig?

"The member replied in the same low tone that, as the question appeared to involve a suspicion that the learned pig might be his half-brother, he must decline answering it.

"Section B – Anatomy and Medicine.
Coach house, Pig and Tinderbox.
President – Dr Toorell. Vice Presidents –
Professors Muff and Nogo.

"Dr Kutankumagen (of Moscow) read to the section a report of a case which had occurred within his own practice, strikingly illustrative of the power of medicine, as exemplified in his successful treatment of a virulent disorder. He had been called in to visit the patient on the 1st of April 1837. He was then labouring under symptoms peculiarly alarming to any medical man. His frame was stout and muscular, his step firm and elastic, his cheeks plump and red, his voice loud, his appetite good, his pulse full and round. He was in the constant habit of eating three meals per diem, and of drinking at least one bottle of wine, and one glass of spirituous liquors diluted with water, in the course of the four-and-twenty hours. He laughed constantly, and in so hearty a manner that it was terrible to hear him. By dint of powerful medicine, low diet and bleeding, the symptoms in the course of three days perceptibly decreased. A rigid perseverance in the same course of treatment for only one week, accompanied with small doses of water gruel, weak broth and barley water, led to their entire disappearance. In the course of a month he was sufficiently recovered to be carried downstairs by two nurses, and to enjoy an airing in a close carriage, supported by soft pillows. At the present moment he was restored so far as to walk about, with the slight assistance of a crutch and a boy. It would perhaps be gratifying to the section to learn that he ate little, drank little, slept little and was never heard to laugh by any accident whatever.

"Dr W.R. Fee, in complimenting the honourable member upon the triumphant cure he had effected, begged to ask whether the patient still bled freely?

"Dr Kutankumagen replied in the affirmative.

"Dr W.R. Fee – And you found that he bled freely during the whole course of the disorder?

"Dr Kutankumagen – Oh dear, yes; most freely.

"Dr Neeshawts supposed, that if the patient had not submitted to be bled with great readiness and perseverance, so extraordinary a cure could never, in fact, have been accomplished. Dr Kutankumagen rejoined, certainly not.

"Mr Knight Bell (MRCS*) exhibited a wax preparation of the interior of a gentleman who in early life had inadvertently swallowed a door key. It was a curious fact that a medical student of dissipated habits, being present at the post-mortem examination, found means to escape unobserved from the room, with that portion of the coats of the stomach upon which an exact model of the instrument was distinctly impressed, with which he hastened to a locksmith of doubtful character, who made a new key from the pattern so shown to him. With this key the medical student entered the house of the deceased gentleman and committed a burglary to a large amount, for which he was subsequently tried and executed.

"THE PRESIDENT wished to know what became of the original key after the lapse of years. Mr Knight Bell replied that the gentleman was always much accustomed to punch, and it was supposed the acid had gradually devoured it.

"DR NEESHAWTS and several of the members were of opinion that the key must have lain very cold and heavy upon the gentleman's stomach.

"MR KNIGHT BELL believed it did at first. It was worthy of remark, perhaps, that for some years the gentleman was troubled with a nightmare, under the influence of which he always imagined himself a wine-cellar door.

"PROFESSOR MUFF related a very extraordinary and convincing proof of the wonderful efficacy of the system of infinitesimal doses, which the section were doubtless aware was based upon the theory that the very minutest amount of any given drug, properly dispersed through the human frame, would be productive of precisely the same result as a very large dose administered in the usual manner. Thus, the fortieth part of a grain of calomel was supposed to be equal to a five-grain calomel pill, and so on in proportion throughout the whole range of medicine. He had tried the experiment in a curious manner upon a publican who had been brought into the hospital with a broken head, and was cured upon the infinitesimal system in the incredibly short space of three months. This man was a hard drinker. He (Professor Muff) had dispersed three drops of rum through a bucket of water, and requested the man to drink the whole. What was the result? Before he had drunk a quart, he was in a state of beastly intoxication, and five other men were made dead drunk with the remainder.

"THE PRESIDENT wished to know whether an infinitesimal dose of soda water would have recovered them? Professor Muff replied that the twenty-fifth part of a teaspoonful, properly administered to each patient, would have sobered him immediately. The President remarked that this was a most important discovery, and he hoped the Lord Mayor and Court of Aldermen would patronize it immediately.

"A MEMBER begged to be informed whether it would be possible to administer, say, the twentieth part of a grain of bread and cheese to all grown-up paupers, and the fortieth part to children, with the same satisfying effect as their present allowance.

"PROFESSOR MUFF was willing to stake his professional reputation on the perfect adequacy of such a quantity of food to the support of human life – in workhouses. The addition of the fifteenth part of a grain of pudding twice a week would render it a high diet.

"PROFESSOR NOGO called the attention of the section to a very extraordinary case of animal magnetism. A private watchman, being merely looked at by the operator from the opposite side of a wide street, was at once observed to be in a very drowsy and languid state. He was followed to his box and, being once slightly rubbed on the palms of the hands, fell into a sound sleep, in which he continued without intermission for ten hours.

"Section C – Statistics.
Hayloft, Original Pig.
President – Mr Woodensconce. Vice Presidents –
Mr Ledbrain and Mr Timbered.

"Mr Slug stated to the section the result of some calculations he had made with great difficulty and labour, regarding the state of infant education among the middle classes of London. He found that, within a circle of three miles from the Elephant and Castle, the following were the names and numbers of children's books principally in circulation:

"*Jack the Giant-Killer*	7,943
Ditto and Beanstalk	8,621
Ditto and Eleven Brothers	2,845
Ditto and Jill	1,998
Total	21,407

"He found that the proportion of Robinson Crusoes to Philip Quarlls was as four and a half to one; and that the preponderance of Valentine and Orsons over Goody Two-Shoeses was as three and an eighth of the former to half a one of the latter; a comparison of Seven Champions with Simple Simons gave the same result.* The ignorance that prevailed was lamentable. One child, on being asked whether he would rather be St George of England or a respectable tallow-chandler, instantly replied, 'Taint George of Ingling.' Another, a little boy of eight years old, was found to be firmly impressed with a belief in the existence of dragons, and openly stated that it was his intention when he grew up to rush forth sword in hand for the deliverance of captive princesses, and the promiscuous slaughter of giants. Not one child among the number interrogated had ever heard of Mungo Park* – some enquiring whether he was at all connected with the black man that swept the crossing, and others whether he was in any way related to the Regent's Park. They had not the slightest conception of the commonest principles of mathematics, and considered Sinbad the Sailor the most enterprising voyager that the world had ever produced.

"A MEMBER, strongly deprecating the use of all the other books mentioned, suggested that Jack and Jill might perhaps be exempted from the general censure, inasmuch as the hero and heroine, in the very outset of the tale, were depicted as going *up* a hill to fetch a pail of water, which was a laborious and useful occupation – supposing the family linen was being washed, for instance.

"MR SLUG feared that the moral effect of this passage was more than counterbalanced by another in a subsequent part of the poem, in which very gross allusion was made to the mode in which the heroine was personally chastised by her mother

"For laughing at Jack's disaster.

Besides, the whole work had this one great fault: *it was not true.*

"THE PRESIDENT complimented the honourable member on the excellent distinction he had drawn. Several other members, too, dwelt upon the immense and urgent necessity of storing the minds of children with nothing but facts and figures; which process the President very forcibly remarked had made them (the section) the men they were.

"MR SLUG then stated some curious calculations respecting the dogs'-meat barrows of London. He found that the total number of small carts and barrows engaged in dispensing provision to the cats and dogs of the metropolis was one thousand, seven hundred and forty-three. The average number of skewers delivered daily with the provender, by each dogs'-meat cart or barrow, was thirty-six. Now, multiplying the number of skewers so delivered by the number of barrows, a total of sixty-two thousand, seven hundred and forty-eight skewers daily would be obtained. Allowing that, of these sixty-two thousand, seven hundred and forty-eight skewers, the odd two thousand, seven hundred and forty-eight were accidentally devoured with the meat by the most voracious of the animals supplied, it followed that sixty thousand skewers per day, or the enormous number of twenty-one millions, nine hundred thousand skewers annually, were wasted in the kennels and dust holes of London; which, if collected and warehoused, would in ten years' time afford a mass of timber more than sufficient for the construction of a first-rate vessel of war for the use of Her Majesty's navy, to be called *The Royal Skewer*, and to become under that name the terror of all the enemies of this island.

"Mr X. Ledbrain read a very ingenious communication, from which it appeared that the total number of legs belonging to the manufacturing population of one great town in Yorkshire was, in round numbers, forty thousand, while the total number of chair and stool legs in their houses was only thirty thousand, which, upon the very favourable average of three legs to a seat, yielded only ten thousand seats in all. From this calculation it would appear – not taking wooden or cork legs into the account, but allowing two legs to every person – that ten thousand individuals (one half of the whole population) were either destitute of any rest for their legs at all, or passed the whole of their leisure time in sitting upon boxes.

"Section D – Mechanical Science.
Coach house, Original Pig.
President – Mr Carter. Vice Presidents –
Mr Truck and Mr Waghorn.

"Professor Queerspeck exhibited an elegant model of a portable railway, neatly mounted in a green case, for the waistcoat pocket. By attaching this beautiful instrument to his boots, any Bank* or public-office clerk could transport himself from his place of residence to his place of business, at the easy rate of sixty-five miles an hour, which, to gentlemen of sedentary pursuits, would be an incalculable advantage.

"The President was desirous of knowing whether it was necessary to have a level surface on which the gentleman was to run.

"PROFESSOR QUEERSPECK explained that City gentlemen would run in trains, being handcuffed together to prevent confusion or unpleasantness. For instance, trains would start every morning at eight, nine and ten o'clock, from Camden Town, Islington, Camberwell, Hackney and various other places in which city gentlemen are accustomed to reside. It would be necessary to have a level, but he had provided for this difficulty by proposing that the best line that the circumstances would admit of should be taken through the sewers which undermine the streets of the metropolis, and which, well lit by jets from the gas pipes which run immediately above them, would form a pleasant and commodious arcade, especially in wintertime, when the inconvenient custom of carrying umbrellas, now so general, could be wholly dispensed with. In reply to another question, Professor Queerspeck stated that no substitute for the purposes to which these arcades were at present devoted had yet occurred to him, but that he hoped no fanciful objection on this head would be allowed to interfere with so great an undertaking.

"MR JOBBA produced a forcing machine on a novel plan, for bringing joint-stock railway shares prematurely to a premium. The instrument was in the form of an elegant gilt weather glass, of most dazzling appearance, and was worked behind, by strings, after the manner of a pantomime trick, the strings being always pulled by the directors of the company to which the machine belonged. The quicksilver was so ingeniously placed that, when the acting directors held shares in their pockets, figures denoting very small expenses and very large returns appeared upon the glass; but the moment the directors parted with these pieces of paper, the estimate of needful expenditure suddenly increased itself to an immense extent, while the statements of certain profits became reduced in the same proportion. Mr Jobba stated that the machine had been in constant requisition for some months past, and he had never once known it to fail.

"A MEMBER expressed his opinion that it was extremely neat and pretty. He wished to know whether it was not liable to accidental derangement? Mr Jobba said that the whole machine was undoubtedly liable to be blown up, but that was the only objection to it.

"PROFESSOR NOGO arrived from the anatomical section to exhibit a model of a safety fire escape, which could be fixed at any time, in less than half an hour, and by means of which, the youngest or most infirm persons (successfully resisting the progress of the flames until it was quite ready) could be preserved if they merely balanced themselves for a few minutes on the sill of their bedroom window, and got into the escape without falling into the street. The Professor stated that the number of boys who had been rescued in the daytime by this machine from houses which were not on fire was almost incredible. Not a conflagration had occurred in the whole of London for many months past to which the escape had not been carried on the very next day, and put in action before a concourse of persons.

"THE PRESIDENT enquired whether there was not some difficulty in ascertaining which was the top of the machine and which the bottom, in cases of pressing emergency.

"PROFESSOR NOGO explained that of course it could not be expected to act quite as well when there was a fire as when there was not a fire; but in the former case he thought it would be of equal service whether the top were up or down."

With the last section our correspondent concludes his most able and faithful report, which will never cease to reflect credit upon him for his scientific attainments, and upon us for our enterprising spirit. It is needless to take a review of the subjects which have been discussed; of the mode in which they have been examined; of the great truths which they have elicited. They are now before the world, and we leave them to read, to consider and to profit.

The place of meeting for next year has undergone discussion and has at length been decided, regard being had to, and evidence being taken upon the goodness of its wines, the supply of its markets, the hospitality of its inhabitants and the quality of its hotels. We hope at this next meeting our correspondent may again be present, and that we may be once more the means of placing his communications before the world. Until that period we have been prevailed upon to allow this number of our miscellany to be retailed to the public, or wholesaled to the trade, without any advance upon our usual price.

We have only to add that the committees are now broken up, and that Mudfog is once again restored to its accustomed tranquillity, that professors and members have had balls, and soirées, and suppers, and great mutual complimentations, and have at length dispersed to their several homes, whither all good wishes and joys attend them, until next year! Signed Boz.*

Full Report of the Second Meeting
of the Mudfog Association for the
Advancement of Everything

I N OCTOBER LAST, we did ourselves the immortal credit of recording, at an enormous expense, and by dint of exertions unparalleled in the history of periodical publication, the proceedings of the Mudfog Association for the Advancement of Everything, which in that month held its first great half-yearly meeting, to the wonder and delight of the whole Empire. We announced at the conclusion of that extraordinary and most remarkable report that when the second meeting of the society should take place, we should be found again at our post, renewing our gigantic and spirited endeavours, and once more making the world ring with the accuracy, authenticity, immeasurable superiority and intense remarkability of our account of its proceedings. In redemption of this pledge, we caused to be dispatched per steam to Oldcastle* (at which place this second meeting of the society was held on the 20th instant), the same superhumanly endowed gentleman who furnished the former report, and who – gifted by nature with transcendent abilities, and furnished by us with a body of assistants scarcely inferior to himself – has forwarded a series of letters, which, for faithfulness of description, power of language, fervour of thought, happiness of expression and importance of subject matter, have no equal in the epistolary literature of any age or country. We give this gentleman's correspondence entire, and in the order in which it reached our office.

"*Saloon of steamer, Thursday night, half-past eight.*
"When I left New Burlington Street* this evening in the hackney cabriolet, number four thousand, two hundred and eighty-five, I experienced sensations as novel as they were oppressive. A sense of the importance of the task I had undertaken, a consciousness that I was leaving London and, stranger still, going somewhere else, a feeling of loneliness and a sensation of jolting, quite bewildered my thoughts, and for a time rendered me even insensible to the presence of my carpet bag and hatbox. I shall ever feel grateful to the driver of a Blackwall omnibus who, by thrusting the pole of his vehicle through the small door of the cabriolet, awakened me from a tumult of imaginings that are wholly indescribable. But of such materials is our imperfect nature composed!

"I am happy to say that I am the first passenger on board, and shall thus be enabled to give you an account of all that happens in the order of its occurrence. The chimney is smoking a good deal, and so are the crew; and the captain, I am informed, is very drunk in a little house upon deck, something like a black turnpike. I should infer from all I hear that he has got the steam up.

"You will readily guess with what feelings I have just made the discovery that my berth is in the same closet with those engaged by Professor Woodensconce, Mr Slug and Professor Grime. Professor Woodensconce has taken the shelf above me, and Mr Slug and Professor Grime the two shelves opposite. Their luggage has already arrived. On Mr Slug's bed is a long tin tube of about three inches in diameter, carefully closed at both ends. What can this contain? Some powerful instrument of a new construction, doubtless."

"*Ten minutes past nine.*

"Nobody has yet arrived, nor has anything fresh come in my way except several joints of beef and mutton, from which I conclude that a good plain dinner has been provided for tomorrow. There is a singular smell below, which gave me some uneasiness at first; but as the steward says it is always there and never goes away, I am quite comfortable again. I learn from this man that the different sections will be distributed at the Black Boy and Stomach Ache, and the Bootjack and Countenance. If this intelligence be true (and I have no reason to doubt it), your readers will draw such conclusions as their different opinions may suggest.

"I write down these remarks as they occur to me, or as the facts come to my knowledge, in order that my first impressions may lose nothing of their original vividness. I shall dispatch them in small packets as opportunities arise."

"*Half-past nine.*
"Some dark object has just appeared upon the wharf. I think it is a travelling carriage."

"*A quarter to ten.*
"No, it isn't."

"*Half-past ten.*
"The passengers are pouring in every instant. Four omnibuses full have just arrived upon the wharf, and all is bustle and activity. The noise and confusion are very great. Cloths are laid in the cabins, and the steward is placing blue plates full of knobs of cheese at equal distances down the centre of the tables. He drops a great many knobs; but, being used to it, picks them up again with great dexterity and, after wiping them on his sleeve, throws them back into the plates. He is a young man of exceedingly prepossessing appearance – either dirty or a mulatto, but I think the former.

"An interesting old gentleman, who came to the wharf in an omnibus, has just quarrelled violently with the porters, and is staggering towards the vessel with a large trunk in his arms. I trust and hope that he may reach it in safety; but the board he has to cross is narrow and slippery. Was that a splash? Gracious powers!

"I have just returned from the deck. The trunk is standing upon the extreme brink of the wharf, but the old gentleman is nowhere to be seen. The watchman is not sure whether he went down or not, but promises to drag for him the first thing tomorrow morning. May his humane efforts prove successful!

"Professor Nogo has this moment arrived with his nightcap on under his hat. He has ordered a glass of cold brandy and water, with a hard biscuit and a basin, and has gone straight to bed. What can this mean?

"The three other scientific gentlemen to whom I have already alluded have come on board, and have all tried their beds, with the exception of Professor Woodensconce, who sleeps in one of the top ones, and can't get into it. Mr Slug, who sleeps in the other top one, is unable to get out of his, and is to have his supper handed up by a boy. I have had the honour to introduce myself to these gentlemen, and we have amicably arranged the order in which we shall retire to rest; which it is necessary to agree upon, because, although the cabin is very comfortable, there is not room for more than one gentleman to be out of bed at a time, and even he must take his boots off in the passage.

"As I anticipated, the knobs of cheese were provided for the passengers' supper, and are now in course of consumption. Your readers will be surprised to hear that Professor Woodensconce has abstained from cheese for eight years, although he takes butter in considerable quantities. Professor Grime, having lost several teeth, is unable, I observe, to eat his crusts without previously soaking them in his bottled porter. How interesting are these peculiarities!"

"*Half-past eleven.*
"Professors Woodensconce and Grime, with a degree of good humour that delights us all, have just arranged to toss for a

bottle of mulled port. There has been some discussion whether the payment should be decided by the first toss or the best out of three. Eventually the latter course has been determined on. Deeply do I wish that both gentlemen could win; but that being impossible, I own that my personal aspirations (I speak as an individual, and do not compromise either you or your readers by this expression of feeling) are with Professor Woodensconce. I have backed that gentleman to the amount of eighteenpence."

"*Twenty minutes to twelve.*
"Professor Grime has inadvertently tossed his half-crown out of one of the cabin windows, and it has been arranged that the steward shall toss for him. Bets are offered on any side to any amount, but there are no takers.

"Professor Woodensconce has just called 'woman';* but the coin, having lodged in a beam, is a long time coming down again. The interest and suspense of this one moment are beyond anything that can be imagined."

"*Twelve o'clock.*
"The mulled port is smoking on the table before me, and Professor Grime has won. Tossing is a game of chance; but on every ground, whether of public or private character, intellectual endowments or scientific attainments, I cannot help expressing my opinion that Professor Woodensconce ought to have come off victorious. There is an exultation about Professor Grime incompatible, I fear, with true greatness."

"*A quarter past twelve.*

"Professor Grime continues to exult, and to boast of his victory in no very measured terms, observing that he always does win, and that he knew it would be a 'head' beforehand, with many other remarks of a similar nature. Surely this gentleman is not so lost to every feeling of decency and propriety as not to feel and know the superiority of Professor Woodensconce? Is Professor Grime insane? Or does he wish to be reminded in plain language of his true position in society, and the precise level of his acquirements and abilities? Professor Grime will do well to look to this."

"*One o'clock.*

"I am writing in bed. The small cabin is illuminated by the feeble light of a flickering lamp suspended from the ceiling; Professor Grime is lying on the opposite shelf on the broad of his back, with his mouth wide open. The scene is indescribably solemn. The rippling of the tide, the noise of the sailors' feet overhead, the gruff voices on the river, the dogs on the shore, the snoring of the passengers and a constant creaking of every plank in the vessel are the only sounds that meet the ear. With these exceptions, all is profound silence.

"My curiosity has been within the last moment very much excited. Mr Slug, who lies above Professor Grime, has cautiously withdrawn the curtains of his berth and, after looking anxiously out, as if to satisfy himself that his companions are asleep, has taken up the tin tube of which I have before spoken, and is regarding it with great interest. What rare mechanical combination can be contained in that mysterious case? It is evidently a profound secret to all."

"*A quarter past one.*
"The behaviour of Mr Slug grows more and more mysterious. He has unscrewed the top of the tube, and now renews his observations upon his companions, evidently to make sure that he is wholly unobserved. He is clearly on the eve of some great experiment. Pray Heaven that it be not a dangerous one; but the interests of science must be promoted, and I am prepared for the worst."

"*Five minutes later.*
"He has produced a large pair of scissors, and drawn a roll of some substance, not unlike parchment in appearance, from the tin case. The experiment is about to begin. I must strain my eyes to the utmost, in the attempt to follow its minutest operation."

"*Twenty minutes before two.*
"I have at length been enabled to ascertain that the tin tube contains a few yards of some celebrated plaster, recommended – as I discover on regarding the label attentively through my eyeglass – as a preservative against seasickness. Mr Slug has cut it up into small portions, and is now sticking it over himself in every direction."

"*Three o'clock.*

"Precisely a quarter of an hour ago we weighed anchor, and the machinery was suddenly put in motion with a noise so appalling that Professor Woodensconce (who had ascended to his berth by means of a platform of carpet bags arranged by himself on geometrical principles) darted from his shelf head foremost and, gaining his feet with all the rapidity of extreme terror, ran wildly into the ladies' cabin, under the impression that we were sinking, and uttering loud cries for aid. I am assured that the scene which ensued baffles all description. There were one hundred and forty-seven ladies in their respective berths at the time.

"Mr Slug has remarked, as an additional instance of the extreme ingenuity of the steam engine as applied to purposes of navigation, that in whatever part of the vessel a passenger's berth may be situated, the machinery always appears to be exactly under his pillow. He intends stating this very beautiful, though simple discovery to the association."

"*Half-past three.*

"We are still in smooth water; that is to say, in as smooth water as a steam vessel ever can be, for, as Professor Woodensconce (who has just woke up) learnedly remarks, another great point of ingenuity about a steamer is that it always carries a little storm with it. You can scarcely conceive how exciting the jerking pulsation of the ship becomes. It is a matter of positive difficulty to get to sleep."

"*Friday afternoon, six o'clock*.
"I regret to inform you that Mr Slug's plaster has proved of no avail. He is in great agony, but has applied several large, additional pieces notwithstanding. How affecting is this extreme devotion to science and pursuit of knowledge under the most trying circumstances!

"We were extremely happy this morning, and the breakfast was one of the most animated description. Nothing unpleasant occurred until noon, with the exception of Doctor Foxey's brown silk umbrella and white hat becoming entangled in the machinery while he was explaining to a knot of ladies the construction of the steam engine. I fear the gravy soup for lunch was injudicious. We lost a great many passengers almost immediately afterwards."

"*Half-past six*.
"I am again in bed. Anything so heart-rending as Mr Slug's sufferings it has never yet been my lot to witness."

"*Seven o'clock*.
"A messenger has just come down for a clean pocket handkerchief from Professor Woodensconce's bag, that unfortunate gentleman being quite unable to leave the deck, and imploring constantly to be thrown overboard. From this man I understand that Professor Nogo, though in a state of utter exhaustion, clings feebly to the hard biscuit and cold brandy and water, under the impression that they will yet restore him. Such is the triumph of mind over matter.

"Professor Grime is in bed, to all appearance quite well; but he *will* eat, and it is disagreeable to see him. Has this gentleman no sympathy with the sufferings of his fellow creatures? If he has, on what principle can he call for mutton chops – and smile?"

"*Black Boy and Stomach Ache, Oldcastle, Saturday noon.* "You will be happy to learn that I have at length arrived here in safety. The town is excessively crowded, and all the private lodgings and hotels are filled with savans* of both sexes. The tremendous assemblage of intellect that one encounters in every street is in the last degree overwhelming.

"Notwithstanding the throng of people here, I have been fortunate enough to meet with very comfortable accommodation on very reasonable terms, having secured a sofa in the first-floor passage at one guinea per night, which includes permission to take my meals in the bar, on condition that I walk about the streets at all other times, to make room for other gentlemen similarly situated. I have been over the out-houses intended to be devoted to the reception of the various sections, both here and at the Bootjack and Countenance, and am much delighted with the arrangements. Nothing can exceed the fresh appearance of the sawdust with which the floors are sprinkled. The forms are of unplaned deal, and the general effect, as you can well imagine, is extremely beautiful."

"*Half-past nine.*

"The number and rapidity of the arrivals are quite bewildering. Within the last ten minutes a stagecoach has driven up to the door, filled inside and out with distinguished characters, comprising Mr Muddlebranes, Mr Drawley, Professor Muff, Mr X. Misty, Mr X.X. Misty, Mr Purblind, Professor Rummun, the Honourable and Reverend Mr Long Eers, Professor John Ketch, Sir William Joltered, Doctor Buffer, Mr Smith (of London), Mr Brown (of Edinburgh), Sir Hookham Snivey and Professor Pumpkinskull. The ten last-named gentlemen were wet through, and looked extremely intelligent."

"*Sunday, two o'clock, p.m.*

"The Honourable and Reverend Mr Long Eers, accompanied by Sir William Joltered, walked and drove this morning. They accomplished the former feat in boots, and the latter in a hired fly. This has naturally given rise to much discussion.

"I have just learnt that an interview has taken place at the Bootjack and Countenance between Sowster, the active and intelligent beadle of this place, and Professor Pumpkinskull, who, as your readers are doubtless aware, is an influential member of the council. I forbear to communicate any of the rumours to which this very extraordinary proceeding has given rise until I have seen Sowster and endeavoured to ascertain the truth from him."

"Half-past six.

"I engaged a donkey chaise shortly after writing the above, and proceeded at a brisk trot in the direction of Sowster's residence, passing through a beautiful expanse of country, with red-brick buildings on either side, and stopping in the marketplace to observe the spot where Mr Kwakley's hat was blown off yesterday. It is an uneven piece of paving, but has certainly no appearance which would lead one to suppose that any such event had recently occurred there. From this point I proceeded – passing the gasworks and tallow-melter's – to a lane which had been pointed out to me as the beadle's place of residence; and before I had driven a dozen yards further, I had the good fortune to meet Sowster himself advancing towards me.

"Sowster is a fat man, with a more enlarged development of that peculiar conformation of countenance which is vulgarly termed a double chin than I remember to have ever seen before. He has also a very red nose, which he attributes to a habit of early rising – so red, indeed, that but for this explanation I should have supposed it to proceed from occasional inebriety. He informed me that he did not feel himself at liberty to relate what had passed between himself and Professor Pumpkinskull, but had no objection to state that it was connected with a matter of police regulation, and added with peculiar significance, 'Never wos sitch times!'

"You will easily believe that this intelligence gave me considerable surprise, not wholly unmixed with anxiety, and that I lost no time in waiting on Professor Pumpkinskull and stating the object of my visit. After a few moments' reflection, the Professor, who, I am bound to say, behaved with the utmost politeness, openly avowed (I mark the passage in italics) *that he had requested Sowster to attend on the Monday morning at the Bootjack and Countenance, to keep off the boys; and that he had further desired that the under-beadle might be stationed, with the same object, at the Black Boy and Stomach Ache!*

"Now I leave this unconstitutional proceeding to your comments and the consideration of your readers. I have yet to learn that a beadle, without the precincts of a church, churchyard or workhouse, and acting otherwise than under the express orders of churchwardens and overseers in council assembled, to enforce the law against people who come upon the parish, and other offenders, has any lawful authority whatever over the rising youth of this country. I have yet to learn that a beadle can be called out by any civilian to exercise a domination and despotism over the boys of Britain. I have yet to learn that a beadle will be permitted by the commissioners of poor-law regulation to wear out the soles and heels of his boots in illegal interference with the liberties of people not proved poor or otherwise criminal. I have yet to learn that a beadle has power to stop up the Queen's highway at his will and pleasure, or that the whole width of the street is not free and open to any man, boy or woman in existence, up to the very walls of the houses – ay, be they Black Boys and Stomach Aches, or Bootjacks and Countenances, I care not."

"*Nine o'clock.*

"I have procured a local artist to make a faithful sketch of the tyrant Sowster, which, as he has acquired this infamous celebrity, you will no doubt wish to have engraved for the purpose of presenting a copy with every copy of your next number. I enclose it. The under-beadle has consented to write his life, but it is to be strictly anonymous.

The Tyrant Sowster.

"The accompanying likeness is of course from the life, and complete in every respect. Even if I had been totally ignorant of the man's real character, and it had been placed before me without remark, I should have shuddered involuntarily. There is an intense malignity of expression in the features, and a baleful ferocity of purpose in the ruffian's eye, which appals and sickens. His whole air is rampant with cruelty, nor is the stomach less characteristic of his demoniac propensities."

"*Monday.*

"The great day has at length arrived. I have neither eyes, nor ears, nor pens, nor ink, nor paper, for anything but the wonderful proceedings that have astounded my senses. Let me collect my energies and proceed to the account.

"Section A – Zoology and Botany.
Front parlour, Black Boy and Stomach Ache.
President – Sir William Joltered. Vice Presidents –
Mr Muddlebranes and Mr Drawley.

"Mr X.X. Misty communicated some remarks on the disappearance of dancing bears from the streets of London, with observations on the exhibition of monkeys as connected with barrel organs. The writer had observed, with feelings of the utmost pain and regret, that some years ago a sudden and unaccountable change in the public taste took place with reference to itinerant bears, who, being discountenanced by the populace, gradually fell off one by one from the streets of the metropolis, until not one remained to create a taste for natural history in the breasts of the poor and uninstructed. One bear, indeed – a brown and ragged animal – had lingered about the haunts of his former triumphs, with a worn and dejected visage and feeble limbs, and had essayed to wield his quarterstaff for the amusement of the multitude; but hunger, and an utter want of any due recompense for his abilities, had at length driven him from the field, and it was only too probable that he had fallen a sacrifice to the rising taste for grease. He regretted to add that a similar, and no less lamentable change had taken place with reference to monkeys. These delightful animals had formerly been almost as plentiful as the organs on the tops of which they were accustomed to sit; the proportion in the year 1829 (it appeared by the parliamentary return) being as one monkey to three organs. Owing, however, to an altered taste in musical instruments, and the substitution, in a great measure, of narrow boxes of music for organs, which left the monkeys nothing to sit upon, this source of public amusement was wholly dried up. Considering it a matter of the deepest importance, in connection with national education, that the people should not lose such opportunities of making themselves acquainted with the manners and customs of two most interesting species of animals, the author submitted that some measures should be immediately taken for the restoration of these pleasing and truly intellectual amusements.

"THE PRESIDENT enquired by what means the honourable member proposed to attain this most desirable end?

"THE AUTHOR submitted that it could be most fully and satisfactorily accomplished if Her Majesty's Government would cause to be brought over to England, and maintained at the public expense, and for the public amusement, such a number of bears as would enable every quarter of the town to be visited – say at least by three bears a week. No difficulty whatever need be experienced in providing a fitting place for the reception of these animals, as a commodious bear garden could be erected in the immediate neighbourhood of both Houses of Parliament; obviously the most proper and eligible spot for such an establishment.

"PROFESSOR MULL doubted very much whether any correct ideas of natural history were propagated by the means to which the honourable member had so ably adverted. On the contrary, he believed that they had been the means of diffusing very incorrect and imperfect notions on the subject. He spoke from personal observation and personal experience, when he said that many children of great abilities had been induced to believe, from what they had observed in the streets, at and before the period to which the honourable gentleman had referred, that all monkeys were born in red coats and spangles, and that their hats and feathers also came by nature. He wished to know distinctly whether the honourable gentleman attributed the want of encouragement the bears had met with to the decline of public taste in that respect, or to a want of ability on the part of the bears themselves?

"Mr X.X. Misty replied that he could not bring himself to believe but that there must be a great deal of floating talent among the bears and monkeys generally; which, in the absence of any proper encouragement, was dispersed in other directions.

"Professor Pumpkinskull wished to take that opportunity of calling the attention of the section to a most important and serious point. The author of the treatise just read had alluded to the prevalent taste for bears' grease as a means of promoting the growth of hair, which undoubtedly was diffused to a very great and (as it appeared to him) very alarming extent. No gentleman attending that section could fail to be aware of the fact that the youth of the present age evinced, by their behaviour in the streets, and at all places of public resort, a considerable lack of that gallantry and gentlemanly feeling which, in more ignorant times, had been thought becoming. He wished to know whether it were possible that a constant outward application of bears' grease by the young gentlemen about town had imperceptibly infused into those unhappy persons something of the nature and quality of the bear. He shuddered as he threw out the remark; but if this theory, on enquiry, should prove to be well founded, it would at once explain a great deal of unpleasant eccentricity of behaviour, which, without some such discovery, was wholly unaccountable.

"The President highly complimented the learned gentleman on his most valuable suggestion, which produced the greatest effect upon the assembly, and remarked that only a week previous he had seen some young gentlemen at a theatre eyeing a box of ladies with a fierce intensity, which nothing but the influence of some brutish appetite could possibly explain. It was dreadful to reflect that our youth were so rapidly verging into a generation of bears.

"After a scene of scientific enthusiasm it was resolved that this important question should be immediately submitted to the consideration of the council.

"THE PRESIDENT wished to know whether any gentleman could inform the section what had become of the dancing dogs?

"A MEMBER replied, after some hesitation, that on the day after three glee-singers* had been committed to prison as criminals by a late most zealous police magistrate of the metropolis, the dogs had abandoned their professional duties and dispersed themselves in different quarters of the town to gain a livelihood by less dangerous means. He was given to understand that since that period they had supported themselves by lying in wait for and robbing blind men's poodles.

"MR FLUMMERY exhibited a twig, claiming to be a veritable branch of that noble tree known to naturalists as the *Shakespeare*, which has taken root in every land and climate, and gathered under the shade of its broad green boughs the great family of mankind. The learned gentleman remarked that the twig had been undoubtedly called by other names in its time; but that it had been pointed out to him by an old lady in Warwickshire, where the great tree had grown, as a shoot of the genuine *Shakespeare*, by which name he begged to introduce it to his countrymen.

"THE PRESIDENT wished to know what botanical definition the honourable gentleman could afford of the curiosity.

"MR FLUMMERY expressed his opinion that it was *a decided plant*.

"SECTION B – DISPLAY OF MODELS AND MECHANICAL SCIENCE.
LARGE ROOM, BOOTJACK AND COUNTENANCE.
President – Mr Mallett. Vice Presidents –
Messrs Leaver and Scroo.

"MR CRINKLES exhibited a most beautiful and delicate machine, of little larger size than an ordinary snuffbox, manufactured entirely by himself, and composed exclusively of steel, by the aid of which more pockets could be picked in one hour than by the present slow and tedious process in four-and-twenty. The inventor remarked that it had been put into active operation in Fleet Street, the Strand and other thoroughfares, and had never been once known to fail.

"After some slight delay, occasioned by the various members of the section buttoning their pockets,

"THE PRESIDENT narrowly inspected the invention, and declared that he had never seen a machine of more beautiful or exquisite construction. Would the inventor be good enough to inform the section whether he had taken any and what means for bringing it into general operation?

"MR CRINKLES stated that, after encountering some pre-liminary difficulties, he had succeeded in putting himself in communication with Mr Fogle Hunter, and other gentlemen connected with the swell mob, who had awarded the invention the very highest and most unqualified approbation. He regretted to say, however, that these distinguished practitioners, in common with a gentleman of the name of Gimlet-Eyed Tommy, and other members of a secondary grade of the profession whom he was understood to represent, entertained an insuperable objection to its being brought into general use, on the ground that it would have the inevitable effect of almost entirely superseding manual labour and throwing a great number of highly deserving persons out of employment.

"The President hoped that no such fanciful objections would be allowed to stand in the way of such a great public improvement.

"Mr Crinkles hoped so too; but he feared that if the gentlemen of the swell mob persevered in their objection, nothing could be done.

"Professor Grime suggested that surely, in that case, Her Majesty's Government might be prevailed upon to take it up.

"Mr Crinkles said that if the objection were found to be insuperable he should apply to Parliament, which he thought could not fail to recognize the utility of the invention.

"The President observed that up to this time Parliament had certainly got on very well without it; but, as they did their business on a very large scale, he had no doubt they would gladly adopt the improvement. His only fear was that the machine might be worn out by constant working.

"Mr Coppernose called the attention of the section to a proposition of great magnitude and interest, illustrated by a vast number of models, and stated with much clearness and perspicuity in a treatise entitled 'Practical suggestions on the necessity of providing some harmless and wholesome relaxation for the young noblemen of England'. His proposition was that a space of ground of not less than ten miles in length and four in breadth should be purchased by a new company, to be incorporated by Act of Parliament, and enclosed by a brick wall of not less than twelve feet in height. He proposed that it should be laid out with highway roads, turnpikes, bridges, miniature villages and every object that could conduce to the comfort and glory of Four-in-hand Clubs,* so that they might be fairly presumed to require no drive beyond it. This delightful retreat would be fitted up with most commodious and extensive stables, for the convenience of such of the nobility and gentry as had a taste for ostlering, and with houses of entertainment furnished in the most expensive and handsome style. It would be further provided with whole streets of door knockers and bell handles of extra size, so constructed that they could be easily wrenched off at night, and regularly screwed on again, by attendants provided for the purpose, every day. There would also be gas lamps of real glass, which could be broken at a comparatively small expense per dozen, and a broad and handsome foot pavement for gentlemen to drive their cabriolets upon when they were humorously disposed – for the full enjoyment of which feat live pedestrians would be procured from the workhouse at a very small charge per head. The place being enclosed, and carefully screened from the intrusion of the public, there would be no objection to gentlemen laying aside any article of their costume that was considered to interfere with a pleasant frolic or, indeed, to their walking about without any costume at all, if they liked that better. In short, every facility of enjoyment would be afforded that the most gentlemanly person could possibly desire. But as even these advantages would be incomplete unless there were some means provided of enabling the nobility and gentry to display their prowess when they sallied forth after dinner, and as some inconvenience might be experienced in the event of their being reduced to the necessity of pummelling each other, the inventor had turned his attention to the construction of an entirely new police force, composed exclusively of automaton figures, which, with the assistance of the ingenious Signor Gagliardi,* of Windmill Street, in the Haymarket, he had succeeded in making with such nicety that a policeman, cab driver or old woman, made upon the principle of the models exhibited, would walk about until knocked down like any real man; nay, more, if set upon and beaten by six or eight noblemen or gentlemen, after it was down, the figure would utter divers groans, mingled with entreaties for mercy, thus rendering the illusion complete and the enjoyment perfect. But the invention did not stop even here; for station houses would be built, containing good beds for noblemen and gentlemen during the night, and in the morning they would repair to a commodious police office, where a pantomimic investigation would take place before the automaton magistrates – quite equal to life – who would fine them in so many counters, with which they would be previously provided for the purpose. This office would be furnished with an inclined plane, for the convenience of any nobleman or gentleman who might wish to bring in his horse as a witness; and the prisoners would be at perfect liberty, as they were now, to interrupt the complainants as much as they pleased, and to make any remarks that they thought proper. The charge for these amusements would amount to very little more than they already cost, and the inventor submitted that the public would be much benefited and comforted by the proposed arrangement.

"PROFESSOR NOGO wished to be informed what amount of automaton police force it was proposed to raise in the first instance.

"MR COPPERNOSE replied that it was proposed to begin with seven divisions of police of a score each, lettered from A to G inclusive. It was proposed that not more than half this number should be placed on active duty, and that the remainder should be kept on shelves in the police office ready to be called out at a moment's notice.

"THE PRESIDENT, awarding the utmost merit to the ingenious gentleman who had originated the idea, doubted whether the automaton police would quite answer the purpose. He feared that noblemen and gentlemen would perhaps require the excitement of threshing living subjects.

"Mr Coppernose submitted that as the usual odds in such cases were ten noblemen or gentlemen to one policeman or cab driver, it could make very little difference in point of excitement whether the policeman or cab driver were a man or a block. The great advantage would be that a policeman's limbs might be all knocked off, and yet he would be in a condition to do duty next day. He might even give his evidence next morning with his head in his hand, and give it equally well.

"Professor Muff – Will you allow me to ask you, sir, of what materials it is intended that the magistrates' heads shall be composed?

"Mr Coppernose – The magistrates will have wooden heads of course, and they will be made of the toughest and thickest materials that can possibly be obtained.

"Professor Muff – I am quite satisfied. This is a great invention.

"Professor Nogo – I see but one objection to it. It appears to me that the magistrates ought to talk.

"Mr Coppernose no sooner heard this suggestion than he touched a small spring in each of the two models of magistrates which were placed upon the table; one of the figures immediately began to exclaim with great volubility that he was sorry to see gentlemen in such a situation, and the other to express a fear that the policeman was intoxicated.

"The section, as with one accord, declared with a shout of applause that the invention was complete; and the President, much excited, retired with Mr Coppernose to lay it before the council. On his return,

"Mr Tickle displayed his newly invented spectacles, which enabled the wearer to discern, in very bright colours, objects at a great distance, and rendered him wholly blind to those immediately before him. It was, he said, a most valuable and useful invention, based strictly upon the principle of the human eye.

"The President required some information upon this point. He had yet to learn that the human eye was remarkable for the peculiarities of which the honourable gentleman had spoken.

"Mr Tickle was rather astonished to hear this, when the President could not fail to be aware that a large number of most excellent persons and great statesmen could see, with the naked eye, most marvellous horrors on West India plantations, while they could discern nothing whatever in the interior of Manchester cotton mills. He must know, too, with what quickness of perception most people could discover their neighbour's faults, and how very blind they were to their own. If the President differed from the great majority of men in this respect, his eye was a defective one, and it was to assist his vision that these glasses were made.

"Mr Blank exhibited a model of a fashionable annual, composed of copperplates, gold leaf and silk boards, and worked entirely by milk and water.

"Mr Prosee, after examining the machine, declared it to be so ingeniously composed, that he was wholly unable to discover how it went on at all.

"Mr Blank – Nobody can, and that is the beauty of it.

"Section C – Anatomy and Medicine.
Barroom, Black Boy and Stomach-Ache.
President – Dr Soemup. Vice Presidents –
Messrs Pessell and Mortair.

"Dr Grummidge stated to the section a most interesting case
of monomania, and described the course of treatment he had
pursued with perfect success. The patient was a married lady
in the middle rank of life, who, having seen another lady at
an evening party in a full suit of pearls, was suddenly seized
with a desire to possess a similar equipment, although her husband's finances were by no means equal to the necessary outlay.
Finding her wish ungratified, she fell sick, and the symptoms
soon became so alarming that he (Dr Grummidge) was called
in. At this period the prominent tokens of the disorder were
sullenness, a total indisposition to perform domestic duties,
great peevishness and extreme languor, except when pearls
were mentioned, at which times the pulse quickened, the eyes
grew brighter, the pupils dilated and the patient, after various
incoherent exclamations, burst into a passion of tears, and
exclaimed that nobody cared for her, and that she wished herself dead. Finding that the patient's appetite was affected in the
presence of company, he began by ordering a total abstinence
from all stimulants, and forbidding any sustenance but weak
gruel; he then took twenty ounces of blood, applied a blister
under each ear, one upon the chest and another on the back;
having done which, and administered five grains of calomel, he

left the patient to her repose. The next day she was somewhat low, but decidedly better, and all appearances of irritation were removed. The next day she improved still further, and on the next again. On the fourth there was some appearance of a return of the old symptoms, which no sooner developed themselves than he administered another dose of calomel, and left strict orders that, unless a decidedly favourable change occurred within two hours, the patient's head should be immediately shaved to the very last curl. From that moment she began to mend, and in less than four-and-twenty hours was perfectly restored. She did not now betray the least emotion at the sight or mention of pearls or any other ornaments. She was cheerful and good-humoured, and a most beneficial change had been effected in her whole temperament and condition.

"MR PIPKIN (MRCS) read a short but most interesting communication in which he sought to prove the complete belief of Sir William Courtenay, otherwise Thom, recently shot at Canterbury,* in the homoeopathic system. The section would bear in mind that one of the homoeopathic doctrines was that infinitesimal doses of any medicine which would occasion the disease under which the patient laboured, supposing him to be in a healthy state, would cure it. Now, it was a remarkable circumstance – proved in the evidence – that the deceased Thom employed a woman to follow him about all day with a pail of water, assuring her that one drop (a purely homoeopathic remedy, the section would observe), placed upon his tongue, after death, would restore him. What was the obvious inference? That Thom, who was marching and countermarching in osier beds and other swampy places, was impressed with a presentiment that he should be drowned; in which case, had his instructions been complied with, he could not fail to have been brought to life again instantly by his own prescription. As it was, if this woman, or any other person, had administered an infinitesimal dose of lead and gunpowder immediately after he fell, he would have recovered forthwith. But unhappily the woman concerned did not possess the power of reasoning by analogy, or carrying out a principle, and thus the unfortunate gentleman had been sacrificed to the ignorance of the peasantry.

"SECTION D – STATISTICS.
OUTHOUSE, BLACK BOY AND STOMACH-ACHE.
President – Mr Slug. Vice Presidents –
Messrs Noakes and Styles.

"MR KWAKLEY stated the result of some most ingenious statistical enquiries relative to the difference between the value of the qualification of several members of Parliament as published to the world, and its real nature and amount. After reminding the section that every member of Parliament for a town or borough was supposed to possess a clear freehold estate of three hundred pounds per annum, the honourable gentleman excited great amusement and laughter by stating the exact amount of freehold property possessed by a column of legislators, in which he had included himself. It appeared from this table that the amount of such income possessed by each was o pounds, o shillings and o pence, yielding an average of the same. (Great laughter.) It was pretty well known that there were accommodating gentlemen in the habit of furnishing new members with temporary qualifications, to the ownership of which they swore solemnly – of course as a mere matter of form. He argued from these data that it was wholly unnecessary for members of Parliament to possess any property at all, especially as when they had none the public could get them so much cheaper.

"Supplementary Section E – Umbugology
and Ditchwateristics.
President – Mr Grub. Vice Presidents –
Messrs Dull and Dummy.

"A paper was read by the secretary descriptive of a bay pony with one eye, which had been seen by the author standing in a butcher's cart at the corner of Newgate Market.* The communication described the author of the paper as having, in the prosecution of a mercantile pursuit, betaken himself one Saturday morning last summer from Somers Town to Cheapside; in the course of which expedition he had beheld the extraordinary appearance above described. The pony had one distinct eye, and it had been pointed out to him by his friend Captain Blunderbore, of the Horse Marines, who assisted the author in his search, that whenever he winked this eye he whisked his tail (possibly to drive the flies off), but that he always winked and whisked at the same time. The animal was lean, spavined* and tottering, and the author proposed to constitute it of the family of *Fitfordogsmeataurious*. It certainly did occur to him that there was no case on record of a pony with one clearly defined and distinct organ of vision, winking and whisking at the same moment.

"Mr Q.J. Snuffletoffle had heard of a pony winking his eye, and likewise of a pony whisking his tail, but whether they were two ponies or the same pony he could not undertake positively to say. At all events, he was acquainted with no authenticated instance of a simultaneous winking and whisking, and he really could not but doubt the existence of such a marvellous pony in opposition to all those natural laws by which ponies were governed. Referring, however, to the mere question of his one organ of vision, might he suggest the possibility of this pony having been literally half asleep at the time he was seen, and having closed only one eye.

"The President observed that, whether the pony was half asleep or fast asleep, there could be no doubt that the association was wide awake, and therefore that they had better get the business over and go to dinner. He had certainly never seen anything analogous to this pony, but he was not prepared to doubt its existence; for he had seen many queerer ponies in his time, though he did not pretend to have seen any more remarkable donkeys than the other gentlemen around him.

"Professor John Ketch* was then called upon to exhibit the skull of the late Mr Greenacre,* which he produced from a blue bag, remarking, on being invited to make any observations that occurred to him, 'that he'd pound it as that 'ere 'spectable section had never seed a more gamerer cove nor he vos'.

"A most animated discussion upon this interesting relic ensued; and, some difference of opinion arising respecting the real character of the deceased gentleman, Mr Blubb delivered a lecture upon the cranium before him, clearly showing that Mr Greenacre possessed the organ of destructiveness to a most unusual extent, with a most remarkable development of the organ of carveativeness. Sir Hookham Snivey was proceeding to combat this opinion, when Professor Ketch suddenly interrupted the proceedings by exclaiming, with great excitement of manner, 'Walker!'

"The President begged to call the learned gentleman to order.

"Professor Ketch – Order be blowed! You've got the wrong un, I tell you. It ain't no e'd at all; it's a coker-nut as my brother-in-law has been a-carvin', to hornament his new baked tatur-stall wots a-comin' down 'ere vile the 'sociation's in the town. Hand over, vill you?

"With these words, Professor Ketch hastily repossessed himself of the coconut, and drew forth the skull, in mistake for which he had exhibited it. A most interesting conversation ensued; but as there appeared some doubt ultimately whether the skull was Mr Greenacre's, or a hospital patient's, or a pauper's, or a man's, or a woman's, or a monkey's, no particular result was obtained.

"I cannot," says our talented correspondent in conclusion, "I cannot close my account of these gigantic researches and sublime and noble triumphs without repeating a bon mot of Professor Woodensconce's, which shows how the greatest minds may occasionally unbend when truth can be presented to listening ears, clothed in an attractive and playful form. I was standing by, when, after a week of feasting and feeding, that learned gentleman, accompanied by the whole body of wonderful men, entered the hall yesterday, where a sumptuous dinner was prepared; where the richest wines sparkled on the board and fat bucks – propitiatory sacrifices to learning – sent forth their savoury odours. 'Ah!' said Professor Woodensconce, rubbing his hands, 'this is what we meet for; this is what inspires us; this is what keeps us together, and beckons us onward; this is the *spread* of science, and a glorious spread it is.'"

The Pantomime of Life

B EFORE WE PLUNGE HEADLONG into this paper, let us at once confess to a fondness for pantomimes – to a gentle sympathy with clowns and Pantaloons – to an unqualified admiration of Harlequins and Columbines* – to a chaste delight in every action of their brief existence, varied and many-coloured as those actions are, and inconsistent though they occasionally be with those rigid and formal rules of propriety which regulate the proceedings of meaner and less comprehensive minds. We revel in pantomimes – not because they dazzle one's eyes with tinsel and gold leaf; not because they present to us, once again, the well-beloved chalked faces and goggle eyes of our childhood; not even because, like Christmas Day, and Twelfth Night, and Shrove Tuesday, and one's own birthday, they come to us but once a year – our attachment is founded on a graver and a very different reason. A pantomime is to us a mirror of life; nay more, we maintain that it is so to audiences generally, although they are not aware of it, and that this very circumstance is the secret cause of their amusement and delight.

Let us take a slight example. The scene is a street: an elderly gentleman, with a large face and strongly marked features, appears. His countenance beams with a sunny smile, and a perpetual dimple is on his broad, red cheek. He is evidently an opulent elderly gentleman, comfortable in circumstances and well-to-do in the world. He is not unmindful of the adornment of his person, for he is richly, not to say gaudily dressed, and that he indulges to a reasonable extent in the pleasures of the table may be inferred from the joyous and oily manner in which he rubs his stomach, by way of informing the audience that he is going home to dinner. In the fullness of his heart, in the fancied security of wealth, in the possession and enjoyment of all the good things of life, the elderly gentleman suddenly loses his footing and stumbles. How the audience roar! He is set upon by a noisy and officious crowd, who buffet and cuff him unmercifully. They scream with delight! Every time the elderly gentleman struggles to get up, his relentless persecutors knock him down again. The spectators are convulsed with merriment! And when at last the elderly gentleman does get up, and staggers away, despoiled of hat, wig and clothing, himself battered to pieces, and his watch and money gone, they are exhausted with laughter, and express their merriment and admiration in rounds of applause.

Is this like life? Change the scene to any real street – to the Stock Exchange, or the City banker's, the merchant's counting house, or even the tradesman's shop. See any one of these men fall – the more suddenly, and the nearer the zenith of his pride and riches, the better. What a wild hallo is raised over his prostrate carcass by the shouting mob; how they whoop and yell as he lies humbled beneath them! Mark how eagerly they set upon him when he is down, and how they mock and deride him as he slinks away. Why, it is the pantomime to the very letter.

Of all the pantomimic dramatis personae, we consider the Pantaloon the most worthless and debauched. Independent of the dislike one naturally feels at seeing a gentleman of his years engaged in pursuits highly unbecoming his gravity and time of life, we cannot conceal from ourselves the fact that he is a treacherous, worldly-minded old villain, constantly enticing his younger companion, the Clown, into acts of fraud or petty larceny, and generally standing aside to watch the result of the enterprise. If it be successful, he never forgets to return for his share of the spoil; but if it turn out a failure, he generally retires with remarkable caution and expedition, and keeps carefully aloof until the affair has blown over. His amorous propensities, too, are eminently disagreeable, and his mode of addressing ladies in the open street at noonday is downright improper, being usually neither more nor less than a perceptible tickling of the aforesaid ladies in the waist, after committing which, he starts back, manifestly ashamed (as well he may be) of his own indecorum and temerity; continuing, nevertheless, to ogle and beckon to them from a distance in a very unpleasant and immoral manner.

Is there any man who cannot count a dozen Pantaloons in his own social circle? Is there any man who has not seen them swarming at the west end of the town on a sunshiny day or a summer's evening, going through the last-named pantomimic feats with as much liquorish energy, and as total an absence of reserve, as if they were on the very stage itself? We can tell upon our fingers a dozen Pantaloons of our acquaintance at this moment – capital Pantaloons, who have been performing all kinds of strange freaks, to the great amusement of their friends and acquaintance, for years past; and who to this day are making such comical and ineffectual attempts to be young and dissolute, that all beholders are like to die with laughter.

Take that old gentleman who has just emerged from the Café de l'Europe in the Haymarket, where he has been dining at the expense of the young man upon town with whom he shakes hands as they part at the door of the tavern. The affected warmth of that shake of the hand, the courteous nod, the obvious recollection of the dinner, the savoury flavour of which still hangs upon his lips are all characteristics of his great prototype. He hobbles away humming an opera tune, and twirling his cane to and fro, with affected carelessness. Suddenly he stops – 'tis at the milliner's window. He peeps through one of the large panes of glass; and, his view of the ladies within being obstructed by the India shawls, directs his attentions to the young girl with the bandbox in her hand, who is gazing in at the window also. See! He draws beside her. He coughs; she turns away from him. He draws near her again; she disregards him. He gleefully chucks her under the chin and, retreating a few steps, nods and beckons with fantastic grimaces, while the girl bestows a contemptuous and supercilious look upon his wrinkled visage. She turns away with a flounce, and the old gentleman trots after her with a toothless chuckle. The Pantaloon to the life!

But the close resemblance which the clowns of the stage bear to those of everyday life is perfectly extraordinary. Some people talk with a sigh of the decline of pantomime, and murmur in low and dismal tones the name of Grimaldi.* We mean no disparagement to the worthy and excellent old man when we say that this is downright nonsense. Clowns that beat Grimaldi all to nothing turn up every day, and nobody patronizes them – more's the pity!

"I know who you mean," says some dirty-faced patron of Mr Osbaldistone's, laying down the *Miscellany* when he has got thus far, and bestowing upon vacancy a most knowing glance, "you mean C. J. Smith as did Guy Fawkes, and George Barnwell at the Garden."* The dirty-faced gentleman has hardly uttered the words, when he is interrupted by a young gentleman in no shirt collar and a Petersham coat. "No, no," says the young gentleman. "He means Brown, King and Gibson, at the 'Delphi."* Now, with great deference both to the first-named gentleman with the dirty face, and the last-named gentleman in the non-existing shirt collar, we do *not* mean either the performer who so grotesquely burlesqued the Popish conspirator,* or the three unchangeables who have been dancing the same dance under different imposing titles, and doing the same thing under various high-sounding names for some five or six years last past. We have no sooner made this avowal than the public, who have hitherto been silent witnesses of the dispute, enquire what on earth it is we *do* mean; and, with becoming respect, we proceed to tell them.

It is very well known to all playgoers and pantomime-seers that the scenes in which a theatrical clown is at the very height of his glory are those which are described in the playbills as "Cheesemonger's shop and crockery warehouse", or "Tailor's shop, and Mrs Queertable's boarding house", or places bearing some such title, where the great fun of the thing consists in the hero's taking lodgings which he has not the slightest intention of paying for, or obtaining goods under false pretences, or abstracting the stock-in-trade of the respectable shopkeeper next door, or robbing warehouse porters as they pass under his window, or, to shorten the catalogue, in his swindling everybody he possibly can, it only remaining to be observed that, the more extensive the swindling is, and the more barefaced the impudence of the swindler, the greater the rapture and ecstasy of the audience. Now it is a most remarkable fact that precisely this sort of thing occurs in real life day after day, and nobody sees the humour of it. Let us illustrate our position by detailing the plot of this portion of the pantomime – not of the theatre, but of life.

The Honourable Captain Fitz-Whisker Fiercy, attended by his livery servant Do'em – a most respectable servant to look at, who has grown grey in the service of the Captain's family – views, treats for and ultimately obtains possession of the unfurnished house, such a number, such a street. All the tradesmen in the neighbourhood are in agonies of competition for the

Captain's custom; the Captain is a good-natured, kind-hearted, easy man and, to avoid being the cause of disappointment to any, he most handsomely gives orders to all. Hampers of wine, baskets of provisions, cartloads of furniture, boxes of jewellery, supplies of luxuries of the costliest description, flock to the house of the Honourable Captain Fitz-Whisker Fiercy, where they are received with the utmost readiness by the highly respectable Do'em; while the Captain himself struts and swaggers about with that compound air of conscious superiority and general bloodthirstiness which a military captain should always, and does most times, wear, to the admiration and terror of plebeian men. But the tradesmen's backs are no sooner turned than the Captain, with all the eccentricity of a mighty mind, and assisted by the faithful Do'em, whose devoted fidelity is not the least touching part of his character, disposes of everything to great advantage; for, although the articles fetch small sums, still they are sold considerably above cost price, the cost to the Captain having been nothing at all. After various manoeuvres, the imposture is discovered, Fitz-Fiercy and Do'em are recognized as confederates, and the police office to which they are both taken is thronged with their dupes.

Who can fail to recognize in this, the exact counterpart of the best portion of a theatrical pantomime – Fitz-Whisker Fiercy by the Clown; Do'em by the Pantaloon; and supernumeraries by the tradesmen? The best of the joke, too, is that the very coal merchant who is loudest in his complaints against the person who defrauded him is the identical man who sat in the centre of the very front row of the pit last night and laughed the most boisterously at this very same thing – and not so well done either. Talk of Grimaldi, we say again! Did Grimaldi, in his best days, ever do anything in this way equal to Da Costa?

The mention of this latter justly celebrated clown reminds us of his last piece of humour, the fraudulently obtaining certain stamped acceptances from a young gentleman in the army. We had scarcely laid down our pen to contemplate for a few moments this admirable actor's performance of that exquisite practical joke, than a new branch of our subject flashed suddenly upon us. So we take it up again at once.

All people who have been behind the scenes, and most people who have been before them, know that in the representation of a pantomime a good many men are sent upon the stage for the express purpose of being cheated, or knocked down, or both. Now, down to a moment ago, we had never been able to understand for what possible purpose a great number of odd, lazy, large-headed men, whom one is in the habit of meeting here and there and everywhere, could ever have been created. We see it all now. They are the supernumeraries in the pantomime of life; the men who have been thrust into it, with no other view than to be constantly tumbling over each other, and running their heads against all sorts of strange things. We sat opposite to one of these men at a supper table only last week. Now we think of it, he was exactly like the gentlemen with the pasteboard heads and faces who do the corresponding business in the theatrical pantomimes; there was the same broad, stolid simper – the same dull leaden eye – the same unmeaning, vacant stare; and whatever was said, or whatever was done, he always came in at precisely the wrong place, or jostled against something that he had not the slightest business with. We looked at the man across the table again and again; and could not satisfy ourselves what race of beings to class him with. How very odd that this never occurred to us before!

We will frankly own that we have been much troubled with the Harlequin. We see Harlequins of so many kinds in the real living pantomime that we hardly know which to select as the proper fellow of him of the theatres. At one time we were disposed to think that the Harlequin was neither more nor less than a young man of family and independent property, who had run away with an opera dancer, and was fooling his life and his means away in light and trivial amusements. On reflection, however, we remembered that Harlequins are occasionally guilty of witty and even clever acts, and we are rather disposed to acquit our young men of family and independent property, generally speaking, of any such misdemeanours. On a more mature consideration of the subject, we have arrived at the conclusion that the Harlequins of life are just ordinary men, to be found in no particular walk or degree, on whom a certain station, or particular conjunction of circumstances, confers the magic wand. And this brings us to a few words on the pantomime of public and political life, which we shall say at once, and then conclude – merely premising in this place that we decline any reference whatever to the Columbine, being in no wise satisfied of the nature of her connection with her particoloured lover, and not feeling by any means clear that we should be justified in introducing her to the virtuous and respectable ladies who peruse our lucubrations.

We take it that the commencement of a session of Parliament is neither more nor less than the drawing-up of the curtain for a grand comic pantomime, and that His Majesty's most gracious speech on the opening thereof may be not inaptly compared to the Clown's opening speech of "Here we are!" "My lords and gentlemen, here we are!" appears, to our mind at least, to be a very good abstract of the point and meaning of the propitiatory address of the ministry. When we remember how frequently this speech is made, immediately after *the change* too, the parallel is quite perfect,* and still more singular.

Perhaps the cast of our political pantomime never was richer than at this day. We are particularly strong in clowns. At no former time, we should say, have we had such astonishing tumblers, or performers so ready to go through the whole of their feats for the amusement of an admiring throng. Their extreme readiness to exhibit, indeed, has given rise to some ill-natured reflections; it having been objected that by exhibiting gratuitously through the country when the theatre is closed, they reduce themselves to the level of mountebanks, and thereby tend to degrade the respectability of the profession. Certainly Grimaldi never did this sort of thing; and though Brown, King and Gibson have gone to the Surrey in vacation time, and Mr C.J. Smith has ruralized at Sadler's Wells, we find no theatrical precedent for a general tumbling through the country, except in the gentleman, name unknown, who threw summersets* on behalf of the late Mr Richardson,* and who is no authority either, because he had never been on the regular boards.

But, laying aside this question, which after all is a mere matter of taste, we may reflect with pride and gratification of heart on the proficiency of our clowns as exhibited in the season. Night after night will they twist and tumble about, till two, three and four o'clock in the morning; playing the strangest antics, and giving each other the funniest slaps on the face that can possibly be imagined, without evincing the smallest tokens of fatigue. The strange noises, the confusion, the shouting and roaring, amid which all this is done, too, would put to shame the most turbulent sixpenny gallery that ever yelled through a boxing night.

It is especially curious to behold one of these clowns compelled to go through the most surprising contortions by the irresistible influence of the wand of office, which his leader or Harlequin holds above his head. Acted upon by this wonderful charm he will become perfectly motionless, moving neither hand, foot nor finger, and will even lose the faculty of speech at an instant's notice; or on the other hand he will become all life and animation if required, pouring forth a torrent of words without sense or meaning, throwing himself into the wildest and most fantastic contortions, and even grovelling on the earth and licking up the dust. These exhibitions are more curious than pleasing; indeed, they are rather disgusting than otherwise, except to the admirers of such things, with whom we confess we have no fellow feeling.

Strange tricks – very strange tricks – are also performed by the Harlequin who holds for the time being the magic wand which we have just mentioned. The mere waving it before a man's eyes will dispossess his brains of all the notions previously stored there, and fill it with an entirely new set of ideas; one gentle tap on the back will alter the colour of a man's coat completely; and there are some expert performers who, having this wand held first on one side and then on the other, will change from side to side, turning their coats at every evolution, with so much rapidity and dexterity that the quickest eye can scarcely detect their motions. Occasionally, the genius who confers the wand wrests it from the hand of the temporary possessor, and consigns it to some new performer; on which occasions all the characters change sides, and then the race and the hard knocks begin anew.

We might have extended this chapter to a much greater length – we might have carried the comparison into the liberal professions – we might have shown, as was in fact our original purpose, that each is in itself a little pantomime with scenes and characters of its own, complete; but, as we fear we have been quite lengthy enough already, we shall leave this chapter just where it is. A gentleman, not altogether unknown as a dramatic poet, wrote thus a year or two ago:

> All the world's a stage,
> And all the men and women merely players,*

and we, tracking out his footsteps at the scarcely worth mentioning little distance of a few millions of leagues behind, venture to add, by way of new reading, that he meant a pantomime, and that we are all actors in the Pantomime of Life.

Some Particulars Concerning a Lion

W E HAVE A GREAT RESPECT for lions in the abstract. In common with most other people, we have heard and read of many instances of their bravery and generosity. We have duly admired that heroic self-denial and charming philanthropy which prompts them never to eat people except when they are hungry, and we have been deeply impressed with a becoming sense of the politeness they are said to display towards unmarried ladies of a certain state. All natural histories teem with anecdotes illustrative of their excellent qualities, and one old spelling book in particular recounts a touching instance of an old lion, of high moral dignity and stern principle, who felt it his imperative duty to devour a young man who had contracted a habit of swearing, as a striking example to the rising generation.

All this is extremely pleasant to reflect upon and, indeed, says a very great deal in favour of lions as a mass. We are bound to state, however, that such individual lions as we have happened to fall in with have not put forth any very striking characteristics, and have not acted up to the chivalrous character assigned them by their chroniclers. We never saw a lion in what is called his natural state, certainly; that is to say, we have never met a lion out walking in a forest, or crouching in his lair under a tropical sun, waiting till his dinner should happen to come by, hot from the baker's. But we have seen some under the influence of captivity and the pressure of misfortune, and we must say that they appeared to us very apathetic, heavy-headed fellows.

The lion at the Zoological Gardens,* for instance. He is all very well; he has an undeniable mane, and looks very fierce; but – Lord bless us! – what of that? The lions of the fashionable world look just as ferocious, and are the most harmless creatures breathing. A box-lobby* lion or a Regent Street animal will put on a most terrible aspect and roar fearfully, if you affront him; but he will never bite and, if you offer to attack him manfully, will fairly turn tail and sneak off. Doubtless these creatures roam about sometimes in herds and, if they meet any especially meek-looking and peaceably disposed fellow, will endeavour to frighten him; but the faintest show of a vigorous resistance is sufficient to scare them even then. These are pleasant characteristics, whereas we make it matter of distinct charge against the zoological lion and his brethren at the fairs that they are sleepy, dreamy, sluggish quadrupeds.

We do not remember to have ever seen one of them perfectly awake, except at feeding time. In every respect we uphold the biped lions against their four-footed namesakes, and we boldly challenge controversy upon the subject.

With these opinions it may be easily imagined that our curiosity and interest were very much excited the other day, when a lady of our acquaintance called on us and resolutely declined to accept our refusal of her invitation to an evening party. "For," said she, "I have got a lion coming." We at once retracted our plea of a prior engagement, and became as anxious to go as we had previously been to stay away.

We went early, and posted ourselves in an eligible part of the drawing room, from whence we could hope to obtain a full view of the interesting animal. Two or three hours passed, the quadrilles began, the room filled; but no lion appeared. The lady of the house became inconsolable – for it is one of the peculiar privileges of these lions to make solemn appointments and never keep them – when all of a sudden there came a tremendous double rap at the street door, and the master of the house, after gliding out (unobserved as he flattered himself) to peep over the banisters, came into the room, rubbing his hands together with great glee, and cried out in a very important voice, "My dear, Mr —— (naming the lion) has this moment arrived."

Upon this, all eyes were turned towards the door, and we observed several young ladies, who had been laughing and conversing previously with great gaiety and good humour, grow extremely quiet and sentimental; while some young gentlemen, who had been cutting great figures in the facetious and small-talk way, suddenly sank very obviously in the estimation of the company, and were looked upon with great coldness and indifference. Even the young man who had been ordered from the music shop to play the pianoforte was visibly affected, and struck several false notes in the excess of his excitement.

All this time there was a great talking outside, more than once accompanied by a loud laugh and a cry of "Oh! Capital! Excellent!" from which we inferred that the lion was jocose, and that these exclamations were occasioned by the transports of his keeper and our host. Nor were we deceived; for when the lion at last appeared, we overheard his keeper, who was a little prim man, whisper to several gentlemen of his acquaintance, with uplifted hands, and every expression of half-suppressed admiration, that —— (naming the lion again) was in *such* cue tonight!

The lion was a literary one. Of course, there were a vast number of people present who had admired his roarings, and were anxious to be introduced to him; and very pleasant it was to see them brought up for the purpose, and to observe the patient dignity with which he received all their patting and caressing. This brought forcibly to our mind what we had so often witnessed at country fairs, where the other lions are compelled to go through as many forms of courtesy as they chance to be acquainted with, just as often as admiring parties happen to drop in upon them.

While the lion was exhibiting in this way, his keeper was not idle, for he mingled among the crowd, and spread his praises most industriously. To one gentleman he whispered some very choice thing that the noble animal had said in the very act of coming upstairs, which, of course, rendered the mental effort still more astonishing; to another he murmured a hasty account of a grand dinner that had taken place the day before, where twenty-seven gentlemen had got up all at once to demand an extra cheer for the lion; and to the ladies he made sundry promises of interceding to procure the majestic brute's sign manual* for their albums. Then there were little private consultations in different corners, relative to the personal appearance and stature of the lion; whether he was shorter than they had expected to see him, or taller, or thinner, or fatter, or younger, or older; whether he was like his portrait, or unlike it; and whether the particular shade of his eyes was black, or blue, or hazel, or green, or yellow, or mixture. At all these consultations the keeper assisted – and, in short, the lion was the sole and single subject of discussion till they sat him down to whist, and then the people relapsed into their old topics of conversation – themselves and each other.

We must confess that we looked forward with no slight impatience to the announcement of supper; for if you wish to see a tame lion under particularly favourable circumstances, feeding time is the period of all others to pitch upon. We were therefore very much delighted to observe a sensation among the guests, which we well knew how to interpret, and immediately afterwards to behold the lion escorting the lady of the house downstairs. We offered our arm to an elderly female of our acquaintance, who – dear old soul! – is the very best person that ever lived, to lead down to any meal; for, be the room ever so small, or the party ever so large, she is sure, by some intuitive perception of the eligible, to push and pull herself and conductor close to the best dishes on the table; we say we offered our arm to this elderly female and, descending the stairs shortly after the lion, were fortunate enough to obtain a seat nearly opposite him.

Of course the keeper was there already. He had planted himself at precisely that distance from his charge which afforded him a decent pretext for raising his voice, when he addressed him, to so loud a key as could not fail to attract the attention of the whole company, and immediately began to apply himself seriously to the task of bringing the lion out, and putting him through the whole of his manoeuvres. Such flashes of wit as he elicited from the lion! First of all, they began to make puns upon a salt cellar, and then upon the breast of a fowl, and then upon the trifle; but the best jokes of all were decidedly on the lobster salad, upon which latter subject the lion came out most vigorously and, in the opinion of the most competent authorities, quite outshone himself. This is a very excellent mode of shining in society, and is founded, we humbly conceive, upon the classic model of the dialogues between Mr Punch and his friend the proprietor, wherein the latter takes all the uphill work and is content to pioneer to the jokes and repartees of Mr P. himself, who never fails to gain great credit and excite much laughter thereby. Whatever it be founded on, however, we recommend it to all lions, present and to come; for in this instance it succeeded to admiration, and perfectly dazzled the whole body of hearers.

When the salt cellar, and the fowl's breast, and the trifle, and the lobster salad were all exhausted, and could not afford standing room for another solitary witticism, the keeper performed that very dangerous feat which is still done with some of the caravan lions, although in one instance it terminated fatally, of putting his head in the animal's mouth and placing himself entirely at its mercy. Boswell* frequently presents a melancholy instance of the lamentable results of this achievement, and other keepers and jackals have been terribly lacerated for their daring. It is due to our lion to state that he condescended to be trifled with, in the most gentle manner, and finally went home with the showman in a hack cab:* perfectly peaceable, but slightly fuddled.

Being in a contemplative mood, we were led to make some reflections upon the character and conduct of this genus of lions as we walked homewards, and we were not long in arriving at the conclusion that our former impression in their favour was very much strengthened and confirmed by what we had recently seen. While the other lions receive company and compliments in a sullen, moody, not to say snarling manner, these appear flattered by the attentions that are paid them; while those conceal themselves to the utmost of their power from the vulgar gaze, these court the popular eye and, unlike their brethren, whom nothing short of compulsion will move to exertion, are ever ready to display their acquirements to the wondering throng. We have known bears of undoubted ability who, when the expectations of a large audience have been wound up to the utmost pitch, have peremptorily refused to dance; well-taught monkeys who have unaccountably objected to exhibit on the slack wire; and elephants of unquestioned genius who have suddenly declined to turn the barrel organ; but we never once knew or heard of a biped lion, literary or otherwise – and we state it as a fact which is highly creditable to the whole species – who, occasion offering, did not seize with avidity on any opportunity which was afforded him of performing to his heart's content on the first violin.

Mr Robert Bolton, the "Gentleman Connected with the Press"

I N THE PARLOUR OF THE GREEN DRAGON, a public house in the immediate neighbourhood of Westminster Bridge, everybody talks politics, every evening, the great political authority being Mr Robert Bolton, an individual who defines himself as "a gentleman connected with the press", which is a definition of peculiar indefiniteness. Mr Robert Bolton's regular circle of admirers and listeners are an undertaker, a greengrocer, a hairdresser, a baker, a large stomach surmounted by a man's head, and placed on the top of two particularly short legs, and a thin man in black, name, profession and pursuit unknown, who always sits in the same position, always displays the same long, vacant face, and never opens his lips, surrounded as he is by most enthusiastic conversation, except to puff forth a volume of tobacco smoke or give vent to a very snappy, loud and shrill *hem!* The conversation sometimes turns upon literature, Mr Bolton being a literary character, and always upon such news of the day as is exclusively possessed by that talented individual. I found myself (of course, accidentally) in the Green Dragon the other evening and, being somewhat amused by the following conversation, preserved it.

"Can you lend me a ten-pound note till Christmas?" enquired the hairdresser of the stomach.

"Where's your security, Mr Clip?"

"My stock-in-trade – there's enough of it, I'm thinking, Mr Thicknesse. Some fifty wigs, two poles, half a dozen head blocks and a dead bruin."

"No, I won't, then," growled out Thicknesse. "I lends nothing on the security of the Whigs* or the Poles either. As for Whigs, they're cheats; as for the Poles, they've got no cash. I never have nothing to do with blockheads, unless I can't awoid it (ironically), and a dead bear's about as much use to me as I could be to a dead bear."

"Well, then," urged the other, "there's a book as belonged to Pope, Byron's *Poems*,* valued at forty pounds, because it's got Pope's identical scratch on the back; what do you think of that for security?"

"Well, to be sure!" cried the baker. "But how d'ye mean, Mr Clip?"

"Mean! Why, that it's got the *hottergruff* of Pope.

"Steal not this book, for fear of hangman's rope;
For it belongs to Alexander Pope.

"All that's written on the inside of the binding of the book; so, as my son says, we're *bound* to believe it."

"Well, sir," observed the undertaker, deferentially, and in a half-whisper, leaning over the table, and knocking over the hairdresser's grog as he spoke, "that argument's very easy upset."

"Perhaps, sir," said Clip, a little flurried, "you'll pay for the first upset afore you thinks of another."

"Now," said the undertaker, bowing amicably to the hairdresser, "I *think*, I says I *think* – you'll excuse me, Mr Clip, I *think*, you see, that won't go down with the present company – unfortunately, my master had the honour of making the coffin of that 'ere Lord's housemaid, not no more nor twenty year ago. Don't think I'm proud on it, gentlemen; others might be; but I hate rank of any sort. I've no more respect for a lord's footman than I have for any respectable tradesman in this room. I may say no more nor I have for Mr Clip! (Bowing.) Therefore, that 'ere lord must have been born long after Pope died. And it's a logical interference to defer, that they neither of them lived at the same time. So what I mean is this here, that Pope never had no book, never seed, felt, never smelt no book (triumphantly) as belonged to that 'ere Lord. And, gentlemen, when I consider how patiently you have 'eared the ideas what I have expressed, I feel bound, as the best way to reward you for the kindness you have exhibited, to sit down without saying anything more – partickler as I perceive a worthier visitor nor myself is just entered. I am not in the habit of paying compliments, gentlemen; when I do, therefore, I hope I strikes with double force."

"Ah, Mr Murgatroyd! What's all this about striking with double force?" said the object of the above remark, as he entered. "I never excuse a man's getting into a rage during winter, even when he's seated so close to the fire as you are. It is very injudicious to put yourself into such a perspiration. What is the cause of this extreme physical and mental excitement, sir?"

Such was the very philosophical address of Mr Robert Bolton, a shorthand writer, as he termed himself – a bit of equivoque passing current among his fraternity, which must give the uninitiated a vast idea of the establishment of the ministerial organ, while to the initiated it signifies that no one paper can lay claim to the enjoyment of their services. Mr Bolton was a young man, with a somewhat sickly and very dissipated expression of countenance. His habiliments were composed of an exquisite union of gentility, slovenliness, assumption, simplicity, *newness* and old age. Half of him was dressed for the winter, the other half for the summer. His hat was of the newest cut, the d'Orsay;* his trousers had been white, but the inroads of mud and ink, etc., had given them a piebald appearance; round his throat he wore a very high black cravat, of the most tyrannical stiffness; while his *tout ensemble* was hidden beneath the enormous folds of an old brown poodle-collared greatcoat, which was closely buttoned up to the aforesaid cravat. His fingers peeped through the ends of his black kid gloves, and two of the toes of each foot took a similar view of society through the extremities of his high-lows.* Sacred to the bare walls of his garret be the mysteries of his interior dress! He was a short, spare man, of a somewhat inferior deportment. Everybody seemed influenced by his entry into the room, and his salutation of each member partook of the patronizing. The hairdresser made way for him between himself and the stomach. A minute afterwards he had taken possession of his pint and pipe. A pause in the conversation took place. Everybody was waiting, anxious for his first observation.

"Horrid murder in Westminster this morning," observed Mr Bolton.

Everybody changed their positions. All eyes were fixed upon the man of paragraphs.

"A baker murdered his son by boiling him in a copper," said Mr Bolton.

"Good Heavens!" exclaimed everybody, in simultaneous horror.

"Boiled him, gentlemen!" added Mr Bolton, with the most effective emphasis. "*Boiled* him!"

"And the particulars, Mr B.," enquired the hairdresser, "the particulars?"

Mr Bolton took a very long draught of porter, and some two or three dozen whiffs of tobacco, doubtless to instil into the commercial capacities of the company the superiority of a gentleman connected with the press, and then said:

"The man was a baker, gentlemen." (Everyone looked at the baker present, who stared at Bolton.) "His victim, being his son, also was necessarily the son of a baker. The wretched murderer had a wife, whom he was frequently in the habit, while in an intoxicated state, of kicking, pummelling, flinging mugs at, knocking down and half-killing while in bed, by inserting in her mouth a considerable portion of a sheet or blanket."

The speaker took another draught, everybody looked at everybody else, and exclaimed, "Horrid!"

"It appears in evidence, gentlemen," continued Mr Bolton, "that on the evening of yesterday, Sawyer the baker came home in a reprehensible state of beer. Mrs S., connubially considerate, carried him in that condition upstairs into his chamber, and consigned him to their mutual couch. In a minute or two she lay sleeping beside the man whom the morrow's dawn beheld a murderer!" (Entire silence informed the reporter that his picture had attained the awful effect he desired.) "The son came home about an hour afterwards, opened the door and went up to bed. Scarcely (gentlemen, conceive his feelings of alarm), scarcely had he taken off his indescribables, when shrieks (to his experienced ear *maternal* shrieks) scared the silence of surrounding night. He put his indescribables on again, and ran downstairs. He opened the door of the parental bedchamber. His father was dancing upon his mother. What must have been his feelings! In the agony of the minute he rushed at his male parent as he was about to plunge a knife into the side of his female. The mother shrieked. The father caught the son (who had wrested the knife from the paternal grasp) up in his arms, carried him downstairs, shoved him into a copper of boiling water among some linen, closed the lid, and jumped upon the top of it, in which position he was found with a ferocious countenance by the mother, who arrived in the melancholy wash house just as he had so settled himself.

"'Where's my boy?' shrieked the mother.

"'In that copper, boiling,' coolly replied the benign father.

"Struck by the awful intelligence, the mother rushed from the house, and alarmed the neighbourhood. The police entered a minute afterwards. The father, having bolted the wash-house door, had bolted himself. They dragged the lifeless body of the boiled baker from the cauldron and, with a promptitude commendable in men of their station, they immediately carried it to the station house. Subsequently, the baker was apprehended while seated on the top of a lamp-post in Parliament Street, lighting his pipe."

The whole horrible ideality of the *Mysteries of Udolpho*,* condensed into the pithy effect of a ten-line paragraph, could not possibly have so affected the narrator's auditory. Silence, the purest and most noble of all kinds of applause, bore ample testimony to the barbarity of the baker, as well as to Bolton's knack of narration; and it was only broken after some minutes had elapsed by interjectional expressions of the intense indignation of every man present. The baker wondered how a British baker could so disgrace himself and the highly honourable calling to which he belonged; and the others indulged in a variety of wonderments connected with the subject; among which not the least wonderment was that which was awakened by the genius and information of Mr Robert Bolton, who, after a glowing eulogium on himself and his unspeakable influence with the daily press, was proceeding, with a most solemn countenance, to hear the pros and cons of the Pope autograph question, when I took up my hat, and left.

Note on the Text

The text in the present edition is based on the first one-volume edition, published in 1880. The spelling and punctuation have been standardized, modernized and made consistent throughout.

Notes

p. 3, *Bentley's Miscellany*: A literary periodical founded by Richard Bentley (1794–1871) in 1836, and of which Dickens himself was the first editor (until 1839). The pieces that make up *The Mudfog Papers* originally appeared in the magazine in 1837–38.

p. 3, *Our Mutual Friend*: The last novel completed by Dickens, published in 1864–65.

p. 3, *Mr Lupton... so unrivalled a teacher*: The English calligrapher Thomas Tomkins (1743–1816) was a writing master at St Paul's School in London. Joseph Hirst Lupton (1836–1905) was a later surmaster (deputy headmaster) of the same institution.

p. 3, *George Bentley*: George Bentley (1828–1895) was the son of Richard Bentley, the original publisher of *Bentley's Miscellany*. This preface was written in 1880 to accompany the first publication of *The Mudfog Papers* in book form.

p. 6, *Limehouse and Ratcliff Highway*: Ratcliff Highway, known today simply as "the Highway", is a road that runs between the City of London and Limehouse in the East End. In the nineteenth century it was synonymous with crime and vice, not least because of a series of vicious killings in 1811 that became known as "the Ratcliff Highway murders".

p. 8, *Whittington*: A reference to the English folk tale about Dick Whittington, a poor orphan who, accompanied by his cat, travels to London and rises to be lord mayor. The character is named after the real-life Richard Whittington (d.1423), who served as lord mayor of London four times.

p. 14, *two-pair-of-stairs' windows*: Meaning a window two floors from the ground. A "pair" is an old-fashioned name for a flight of stairs.

p. 14, *Captain Manby's apparatus*: The English sea captain George William Manby (1765–1854) was the inventor of the "Manby Mortar", a device that fired a line from the shore to a sinking ship, enabling crew and passengers to be brought to safety.

p. 16, *seventy-four pounder*: A cannon firing shot of this weight.

p. 16, *eight-day clock*: A clock that only needs to be wound once every eight days.

p. 19, *court card*: A king, queen or jack in a deck of playing cards.

p. 20, *Life Guardsman's sabre*: The Life Guards is the household division of the British army, the troops employed to protect the king or queen.

p. 26, *like the anonymous vessel... till next day*: In the poem 'The Bay of Biscay' by the Irish writer Andrew Cherry (1762–1812), the speaker describes how he and his shipmates are forced to weather an overnight storm in the notoriously tempestuous gulf between the western coast of France and the northern coast of Spain: "The night both drear and dark, / Our poor devoted bark, / Till next day, there she lay, / In the Bay of Biscay O!"

p. 32, *Full Report... Advancement of Everything*: This piece and the one that follows are intended as satires on the British Association for the Advancement of Science, founded in 1831, an organization regularly ridiculed in the press as the "British Ass". The correspondent's reports that constitute the two stories are parodies of the accounts of the British Association's meetings that appeared in the literary magazine the *Athenaeum*.

p. 45, *'The Industrious Fleas'*: The Extraordinary Exhibition of the Industrious Fleas was a flea circus on Regent Street, which opened in 1832. A flea circus was a sideshow in which real insects were made to perform feats such as pulling miniature chariots, rowing miniature boats and fighting duels with one another.

p. 48, *M. Garnerin*: André-Jacques Garnerin (1769–1823), pioneer of the parachute.

p. 48, *Vauxhall Gardens*: Pleasure garden in Kennington, on the south bank of the Thames.

p. 49, *Somers Town*: An area of north London.

p. 52, *MRCS*: Member of the Royal College of Surgeons.

p. 55, *He found that... Simple Simons gave the same result*: *The Hermit: Or, the Unparalleled Sufferings and Surprising Adventures of Mr Philip Quarll, an Englishman* (1727) was a popular adventure story, generally attributed to Peter Longueville, about the eponymous Quarll's fifty years of isolation on a South Sea island. As this description suggests, it was highly derivative of *Robinson Crusoe* (1719) by Daniel Defoe (1660–1731). *Valentine and Orson* is a medieval French romance about two twins separated at birth, one of whom is raised as a knight, the other of whom is raised by bears. It was known to British readers in several English versions, the earliest of which dates from around 1550. *The History of Little Goody Two-Shoes*, a variation on the Cinderella legend, was published anonymously in 1765 by John Newbery (1713–67), "the Father of Children's Literature", and became one of the best-known children's stories of its day. "Seven Champions" probably refers to *The Famous Historie of the Seaven Champions of Christendom* (1596) by Richard Johnson (1573–c.1659), which tells the stories of seven patron saints of European countries, including St George, patron saint of England. 'Simple Simon' is a traditional English nursery rhyme.

p. 56, *Mungo Park*: Mungo Park (1771–1806), Scottish explorer of Africa, famous for following the course of the Niger River.

p. 58, *Bank*: The Bank of England, in the City of London.

p. 62, *Boz*: The pseudonym used by Dickens in his early writings.

p. 63, *Oldcastle*: Possibly the town of this name in County Meath, Ireland.

p. 64, *New Burlington Street*: Off Regent Street in the West End of London. New Burlington Street was the location of the office of Richard Bentley, the publisher of *Bentley's Miscellany*.

p. 68, *has just called 'woman'*: According to Dickens himself in the second chapter of *The Pickwick Papers*, the dragon depicted on a gold sovereign being slain by St George was referred to as a woman: "'Not worth while splitting a guinea,' said the stranger, 'toss who shall pay for both – I call; you spin – first time – woman – woman – bewitching woman,' and down came the sovereign with the dragon (called by courtesy a woman) uppermost."

p. 73, *savans*: "Savan" is an old spelling of "savant", meaning a learned and scholarly person.

p. 82, *glee singers*: A glee was an English song for at least three men's voices, usually unaccompanied, popular in the eighteenth and nineteenth centuries.

p. 85, *Four-in-hand Clubs*: A four-in-hand was a carriage driven by horses and controlled by one person. The eighteenth-century "Four-in-hand Club" was made up of reckless, well-to-do young men who would bribe carriage drivers to let them take the reins of their vehicles and drive them at great speeds. By the nineteenth century recreational driving had evolved into a respectable leisure pursuit, and many membership clubs existed.

p. 86, *Signor Gagliardi*: Apparently the owner of a real exhibition of mechanical figures in the period. One notice for this spectacle boasted that it was a "Splendid mechanical museum of 200 automaton figures", in which were represented "His late Majesty William IV, Queen Victoria the 1st and her most gracious mother the Duchess of Kent, as they appeared in their box at Her Majesty's Theatre, on the 18th of July, 1837".

p. 91, *Sir William Courtenay... recently shot at Canterbury*: Born in Cornwall, John Nichols Thom (1799–1838) was an imposter who assumed the name of Sir William Courtenay and claimed the earldom of Devon. An eccentric and outlandish figure, he gained something of a following and stood for Parliament in Canterbury, though failed to win a seat. He was shot and killed in a fight between his band of supporters, which consisted mainly of disgruntled rural labourers and artisans, and some soldiers at Bossenden Wood in Kent.

p. 93, *Newgate Market*: A meat market in the City of London, demolished in 1869.

p. 94, *spavined*: Bone spavin is a form of osteoarthritis of a horse's hock, resulting in lameness.

p. 94, *Professor John Ketch*: Named after Jack Ketch (d.1686), executioner under Charles II.

p. 94, *the late Mr Greenacre*: James Greenacre (1785–1837), known as the "Edgware Road murderer", killed his fiancée and was hanged at Newgate on 2nd May 1837.

p. 97, *Pantaloons... Harlequins and Columbines*: Pantaloon, Harlequin and Columbine were stock characters from the Italian *commedia dell'arte*, a form of comic theatre popular from the sixteenth to the eighteenth century. Along with two other characters, Clown and Pierrot, they became part of the English pantomime tradition known as the harlequinade, acting out the same basic plot in which Pantaloon, the father of Columbine, attempts to separate his daughter from her lover, Harlequin.

p. 101, *Grimaldi*: Joseph Grimaldi (1778–1837) was a famous Regency actor and comedian, best remembered for his performances as the Clown in the harlequinade, a role with which he became synonymous. He wrote an autobiography that was edited (and in effect rewritten) for publication by Dickens himself in 1838.

p. 101, *C.J. Smith as did Guy Fawkes, and George Barnwell at the Garden*: The story of Guy Fawkes and the 1605 Gunpowder Plot to destroy Parliament was the subject of a pantomime, titled *Harlequin and Guy Fawkes, or, the Fifth of November*, performed at the Theatre Royal, Covent Garden in 1835. Another pantomime from around the same time, *Harlequin and George Barnwell, or, The London 'Prentice*, seems to have been a comic send-up of playwright George Lillo's (*c*.1693–1739) tragedy *The London Merchant,*

or, The History of George Barnwell, first performed in 1731.
C.J. Smith was an actor involved in both productions.

p. 101, *Brown, King and Gibson, at the 'Delphi*: Apparently a famous trio of performers of the period. The Adelphi Theatre is on the Strand in London.

p. 101, *Popish conspirator*: Guy Fawkes and his fellow would-be terrorists were Catholic fanatics.

p. 106, *immediately after the change too, the parallel is quite perfect*: Traditionally, the harlequinade occurred at the end of a pantomime or other theatrical presentation, which consisted of an entirely unrelated story and characters. The change from one to the other was signified by an extravagant transition scene, in which the characters from the first play were magically transformed into the stock figures of the harlequinade. Dickens is here comparing this spectacle to a change of government resulting from a general election.

p. 107, *summersets*: An old spelling of "summersaults".

p. 107, *the late Mr Richardson*: The actor and impresario John Richardson (1766–1836), who was the founder of an itinerant fairground theatre that performed in and around London. Dickens provides a description of Richardson's Theatre in 'Greenwich Fair' in *Sketches by Boz* (1836).

p. 109, *All the world's a stage, / And all the men and women merely players*: The opening words of Jaques's famous speech in Shakespeare's *As You Like It*, Act II, Sc. 7.

p. 111, *the Zoological Gardens*: A reference to the zoo in London's Regent's Park, established in 1826 by the

Zoological Society of London. Originally accessible only to members of the society, it opened to the public in 1847.

p. 111, *box-lobby*: The lobby of a theatre.

p. 114, *sign manual*: Autograph. The term "sign manual" usually refers to the signature of the sovereign.

p. 116, *Boswell*: James Boswell (1740–95), Scottish biographer of the English lexicographer and writer Samuel Johnson (1709–84).

p. 116, *hack cab*: A hackney carriage, the official name for a taxi.

p. 119, *the Whigs*: One of the two political parties in Parliament in the first half of the nineteenth century (the other being the Tories). In this period the Whigs stood for the interests of industrialists, supporting free trade religious dissenters and those seeking constitutional and social reforms.

p. 119, *there's a book as belonged to Pope, Byron's Poems*: The point being that this is impossible, since the Augustan poet Alexander Pope (1688–1744) died over forty years before the celebrated Romantic poet George Gordon, Lord Byron (1788–1824) was born.

p. 121, *d'Orsay*: A kind of top hat made with beaver fur fashionable in the early nineteenth century.

p. 121, *high-lows*: Boots worn by military personnel.

p. 124, *Mysteries of Udolpho*: A Gothic novel by Ann Radcliffe (1764–1823), one of the pioneers of the form, published in 1794 and characterized by suspense, sensational incidents of horror and apparently supernatural occurrences.

Extra Material

on

Charles Dickens's

The Mudfog Papers

Charles Dickens's Life

Charles John Huffam Dickens was born in Portsmouth on 7th *First Years*
February 1812 to John Dickens and Elizabeth Dickens, née Barrow.
His father worked as a navy payroll clerk at the local dockyard,
before transferring and moving his family to London in 1814,
and then to Kent in 1817. It seems that this period possessed
an idyllic atmosphere for ever afterwards in Dickens's mind.
Much of his childhood was spent reading and rereading the
books in his father's library, which included *Robinson Crusoe*,
The Vicar of Wakefield, *Don Quixote*, Fielding, Smollett and
the *Arabian Nights*. He was a promising, prize-winning pupil
at school, and generally distinguished by his cleverness, sensitiv-
ity and enthusiasm, although unfortunately this was tempered
by his frail and sickly constitution. It was at this time that he
also had his first experience of what would become one of the
abiding passions in his life: the theatre. Sadly, John Dickens's
finances had become increasingly unhealthy, a situation which
was worsened when he was transferred to London in 1822. This
relocation, which entailed a termination in his schooling, dis-
tressed Charles, though he slowly came to be fascinated with
the teeming, squalid streets of London.

In London, however, family finances continued to plummet *Bankruptcy*
until the Dickenses were facing bankruptcy. A family connection, *and the*
James Lamert, offered to employ Charles at the Warren's Blacking *Warehouse*
Warehouse, which he was managing, and Dickens started working
there in February 1824. He spent between six months and a year
there, and the experience would prove to have a profound and
lasting effect on him. The work was drudgery – sealing and label-
ling pots of black paste all day – and his only companions were
uneducated working-class boys. His discontent at the situation was
compounded by the fact that his talented older sister was sent to
the Royal Academy of Music, while he was left in the warehouse.

John Dickens was finally arrested for debt and taken to Mar-
shalsea Prison in Southwark on 20th February 1824, his wife and

children (excluding Charles) moving in with him in order to save money. Meanwhile, Charles found lodgings with an intimidating old lady called Mrs Roylance (on whom he apparently modelled Mrs Pipchin in *Dombey and Son*) in Little College Street, later moving to Lant Street in Borough, which was closer to the prison. At the end of May 1824, John Dickens was released, and gradually paid off creditors as he attempted to start a new life for himself and his family. However, for some time afterwards Charles reluctantly pursued his employment at the blacking factory, as it seems his mother was unwilling to take him out of it, and even tried to arrange for him to return after he did leave. It appears that he was only removed from the warehouse after his father had quarrelled with James Lamert. The stint at the blacking factory was so profoundly humiliating for Dickens that throughout his life he apparently never mentioned this experience to any of those close to him, revealing it only in a fragment of a memoir written in 1848 and presented to his biographer John Forster: "No words can express the secret agony of my soul as I sunk into this companionship, compared these everyday associates with those of my happier childhood, and felt my early hopes of growing up to be a learned and distinguished man crushed in my breast."

School and Work in London   Fortunately he was granted some respite from hard labour when he was sent to be educated at the Wellington House Academy on Hampstead Road. Although the standard of teaching he received was apparently mediocre, the two years he spent at the school were idyllic compared to his warehouse experience, and Charles took advantage of them by making friends his own age and participating in school drama. Regrettably he had to leave the Academy in 1827, when the family finances were in turmoil once again. He found employment as a junior clerk in a solicitor's office, a job that, although routine and somewhat unfulfilling, enabled Dickens to become familiar with the ways of the London courts and the jargon of the legal profession – which he would later frequently lampoon in his novels. On reaching his eighteenth birthday, Dickens enrolled as a reader at the British Museum, determined to make up for the inadequacies of his education by studying the books in its collection, and taught himself shorthand in the hope of taking on journalistic work.

In less than a year he set himself up as a freelance law reporter, initially covering the civil law courts known as Doctors' Commons – which he did with some brio, though he found it slightly tedious – and in 1831 advanced to the press gallery of the House of Commons. His reputation as a reporter was growing steadily, and in 1834 he joined the staff of the *Morning Chronicle*, one of the leading daily newspapers. During this period, he observed and commented on some of the most socially significant debates of the time, such as the Reform Act of 1832, the Factory Act of 1833 and the Poor Law Amendment Act of 1834.

In 1829, he fell in love with the flirtatious and beautiful Maria Beadnell, the daughter of a wealthy banker, and he seems to have remained fixated on her for several years, although she rebuffed his advances. This disappointment spurred him on to achieve a higher station in life, and – after briefly entertaining the notion of becoming an actor – he threw himself into his work and wrote short stories in his spare time, which he had published in magazines, although without pay.

First Love

Soon enough his work for the *Morning Chronicle* was not limited to covering parliamentary matters: in recognition of his capacity for descriptive writing, he was encouraged to write reviews and sketches, and cover important meetings, dinners and election campaigns – which he reported on with enthusiasm. Written under the pseudonym "Boz", his sketches on London street life – published in the *Morning Chronicle* and then also in its sister paper, the *Evening Chronicle* – were highly rated and gained a popular following. Things were also looking up in Dickens's personal life, as he fell in love with Catherine Hogarth, the daughter of the editor of the *Evening Chronicle*: they became engaged in May 1835, and married on 2nd April 1836 at St Luke's Church in Chelsea, honeymooning in Kent afterwards. At this time his literary career began to gain momentum: first his writings on London were compiled under the title *Sketches by Boz* and printed in an illustrated two-volume edition, and then, just a few days before his wedding, *The Pickwick Papers* began to be published in monthly instalments – becoming the best-selling serialization since Lord Byron's *Childe Harold's Pilgrimage*.

Marriage and First Major Publication

At the end of 1836, Dickens resigned from the *Morning Chronicle* to concentrate on his literary endeavours, and met John Forster, who was to remain a lifelong friend. He helped Dickens to manage the business and legal side of his life, as well as acting as a trusted literary adviser and biographer. Forster's acumen for resolving complex situations was particularly welcome at this point, since, following the resounding success of *The Pickwick Papers*, Dickens had over-committed himself to a number of projects, with newspapers and publishers eager to capitalize on the latest literary sensation, and the deals and payments agreed no longer reflected his stature as an author.

Success

In January 1837, Catherine gave birth to the couple's first child, also called Charles, which prompted the young Dickens family to move from their lodgings in Furnival's Inn in Holborn to a house on 48 Doughty Street. The following month *Oliver Twist* started appearing in serial form in *Bentley's Miscellany*, which lifted the author's name to new heights. This period of domestic bliss and professional fulfilment was tragically interrupted when Catherine's sister Mary suddenly died in May at the age of seventeen. Dickens was devastated and had to interrupt work on *The Pickwick Papers* and *Oliver Twist*; this event would have a deep impact on his world view and his art. But his literary productivity would soon continue unabated; hot on the tail of *Oliver Twist* came *Nicholas Nickleby* (1838–39) and *The Old Curiosity Shop* (1840–41). By this stage, he was the leading author of the day, frequenting high society and meeting luminaries such as his idol, Thomas Carlyle. Consequently he moved to a grand Georgian house near Regent's Park, and frequently holidayed in a house in Broadstairs in Kent.

Whereas his previous novels had all more or less followed his successful formula of comedy, melodrama and social satire, Dickens opted for a different approach for his next major work, *Barnaby Rudge*, a purely historical novel. He found the writing of this book particularly arduous, so he decided that after five years of intensive labour he needed a sabbatical, and persuaded his publishers Chapman and Hall to grant him a year's leave with a monthly advance of £150 on his future earnings. During this year he would visit America and keep a notebook on his travels, with a view to getting it published on his return.

First Visit to America   Dickens journeyed by steamship to Halifax, Nova Scotia, accompanied by his wife, in January 1842, and the couple would spend almost five months travelling around North America, visiting cities such as Boston, New York, Philadelphia, Cincinnati, Louisville, Toronto and Montreal. He was greeted by crowds of enthusiastic well-wishers wherever he went, and met countless important figures such as Henry Wadsworth Longfellow, Edgar Allan Poe and President John Tyler, but after the initial exhilaration of this fanfare he found it exhausting and overwhelming. The trip also brought about its share of disillusionment: having cherished romantic dreams of America being free from the corruption and snobbery of Europe, he was increasingly appalled by certain aspects of the New World, such as slavery, the treatment of prisoners and, perhaps most of all, the refusal of America to sign an international copyright agreement to prevent his works being pirated in America. He wrote articles and made speeches condemning these practices, which resulted in a considerable amount of press hostility.

Having returned to England in the summer of 1842, he published his record of the trip under the title of *American Notes* and the first instalment of *Martin Chuzzlewit* later that year. Unfortunately neither of the two were quite as successful as he or his publishers would have hoped, although Dickens believed *Martin Chuzzlewit* (1842–44) was his finest work to date. During this period, Dickens started taking a greater interest in political and social issues, particularly in the treatment of children employed in mines and factories, and in the "ragged school" movement, which provided free education for destitute children. He became acquainted with the millionaire philanthropist Angela Burdett-Coutts, and persuaded her to give financial support to a school in London. In 1843, he decided to write a seasonal tale which would highlight the plight of the poor, publishing *A Christmas Carol* to great popular success in December 1843. The following year Dickens decided to leave Chapman and Hall, as his relations with them had become increasingly strained, and persuaded his printer Bradbury and Evans to become his new publisher. *Back Home*

In July 1844 Dickens relocated his entire family to Genoa in order to escape London and find new sources of inspiration – and also because life in Italy was considerably cheaper. Dickens, although at first taken aback by the decay of the Ligurian capital, appears to have been fascinated by this new country and a quick learner of its language and customs. He did not write much there, apart from another Christmas book, *The Chimes*, the publication of which occasioned a brief return to London. In all the Dickenses remained in Italy for a year, travelling around the country for three months in early 1845, before returning to England in July of that year. *Move to Genoa*

In Italy, he discovered that he was apparently able mesmerically to alleviate the condition of Augusta de la Rue, the wife of a Swiss banker, who suffered from anxiety and nervous spasms. This treatment required him to spend a lot of time alone with her, and unsurprisingly Catherine was not best pleased by this turn of events. She was also worn out by the burden of motherhood: they were becoming a large family, and would eventually have a total of ten children. Catherine's sister Georgina therefore began to help out with the children. Georgina was in many ways similar to Mary, whose death had so devastated Dickens, and she became involved with Dickens's various projects.

Back in London, Dickens took part in amateur theatrical productions, and took on the task of editing the *Daily News*, a new national newspaper owned by Bradbury and Evans. However, he had severely underestimated the work involved in editing the publication and resigned after seventeen issues, though he did continue to write contributions, including a series of 'Travelling Letters' – later collected in *Pictures from Italy* (1846).

More Travels   Perhaps to escape the aftermath of his resignation from the *Daily*
Abroad   *News* and to focus on composing his next novel, Dickens moved his family to Lausanne in Switzerland. He enjoyed the clean, quiet and beautiful surroundings, as well as the company of the town's fellow English expatriates. He also managed to write fiction: another Christmas tale entitled *The Battle of Life* and, more significantly, the beginning of *Dombey and Son*, which began serialization in September 1846 and was an immediate success.

It was also at this point that his publisher launched a series of cheap editions of his works, in the hope of tapping into new markets. Dickens returned to London, and resumed his normal routine of socializing, amateur theatricals, letter-writing and public speaking, and also became deeply involved in charitable work, such as setting up and administering a shelter for homeless women, which was funded by Miss Burdett-Coutts. *The Haunted Man*, another Christmas story, appeared in 1848, and was followed by his next major novel, *David Copperfield* (1849–50), which received rapturous critical acclaim.

Household   *Household Words* was set up at this time, a popular magazine
Words   founded and edited by Dickens himself. The magazine contained fictional work by not only Dickens, but also contributors such as Gaskell and Wilkie Collins, and articles on social issues. Dickens continued with his amateur theatricals, which proved a welcome distraction, since Catherine was quite seriously ill, as was his father, who died shortly afterwards. This was followed by the sudden death of his eight-month-old daughter Dora.

The Dickenses moved house again in November 1851, this time to Tavistock House in Tavistock Square. Since it was in a dilapidated state, renovation was necessary, and Dickens personally supervised every detail of this, from the installation of new plumbing to the choice of wallpaper. *Bleak House* (1852–53), his next publication, sold well, though straight after finishing it, Dickens was in desperate need of a break. He went on holiday in France with his family, and then toured Italy with Wilkie Collins and the painter Augustus Egg. After his return to London, Dickens gave a series of public readings to larger audiences than he had been accustomed to. Dickens's histrionic talents thrived in this context and the readings were a triumph, encouraging the author to repeat the exercise throughout his career – indeed, this became a lucrative venture, with Dickens employing his friend Arthur Smith as his booking agent.

During this period Dickens's stance on current politics and society became increasingly critical, which manifested itself in the numerous satirical essays he penned and the darker, more trenchant outlook of *Bleak House* and the two novels that followed, *Hard Times* (1854) and *Little Dorrit* (1855–57). In March 1856, Dickens bought Gad's Hill Place, near Rochester, for use as a country home. He had admired it during childhood country walks with his father, who had told him he might eventually own it if he were very hard-working and persevering.

However, this acquisition of a permanent home was not accompanied by domestic felicity, as by this point Dickens's marriage was in crisis. Relations between Dickens and his wife had been worsening for some time, but it all came to a head when he became acquainted with a young actress by the name of Ellen Ternan and apparently fell in love with her. The affair may never have been consummated, but Dickens involved himself with Ellen and her family's life to an extent which alarmed Catherine, just as she had been alarmed by the excessive attentions he had paid to Mme de la Rue in Genoa. Soon enough, Dickens moved into a separate bedroom in their house, and in May 1858, Dickens and his wife formally separated. This gave rise to a flurry of speculation, including rumours that Dickens was involved in a relationship with the young actress, or even worse, his sister-in-law, Georgina Hogarth, who had opted to continue living with Dickens instead of with her sister. It seemed that some of these allegations may have originated from the Hogarths, his wife's immediate family, and Dickens reacted to this by forcing them to sign a retraction, and by issuing a public statement – against his friends' advice – in *The Times* and *Household Words*. Furthermore, in August of that year one of Dickens's private letters was leaked to the press, which placed the blame for the breakdown of their marriage entirely on Catherine's shoulders, accused her of being a bad mother and insinuated that she was mentally unstable. After some initial protests, Catherine made no further effort to defend herself, and lived a quiet life until her death twenty years later. She apparently never met Dickens again, but never stopped caring about him, and followed his career and publications assiduously.

This conflict in Dickens's personal affairs also had an effect on his professional life: in 1859 the author fell out with Bradbury and Evans after they had refused to run another statement about his private life in one of their publications, the satirical magazine

The End of the Marriage

All the Year Round

143

Punch. This led him to transfer back to Chapman and Hall and to found a new weekly periodical *All the Year Round*. His first contribution to the magazine was his highly successful second historical novel, *A Tale of Two Cities* (1859), an un-Dickensian work in that it was more or less devoid of comical and satirical elements. *All the Year Round* – which focused more on fiction and less on journalistic pieces than its predecessor – maintained very healthy circulation figures, especially as the second novel to be serialized was the tremendously popular *The Woman in White* by Wilkie Collins, who became a regular collaborator. Dickens also arranged with the New York publisher J.M. Emerson & Co. for his journal to appear across the Atlantic. In December 1860, Dickens began to serialize what would become one of his best-loved novels, the deeply autobiographical *Great Expectations* (1860–61).

Our Mutual Friend   Between the final instalment of *Great Expectations* and the first instalment of his next and final completed novel, *Our Mutual Friend*, there was an uncharacteristically long three-year gap. This period was marked by two deaths in the family in 1863: that of his mother – which came as a relief more than anything, as she had been declining into senility for some time, and Dickens's feeling for her were ambivalent at best – and that of his second son, Walter – for whom Dickens grieved much more deeply. He chewed over ideas for *Our Mutual Friend* for at least two years and only began seriously composing it in early 1864, with serialization beginning in May. Although the book is now widely considered a masterpiece, it met with a tepid reception at the time, as readers did not entirely understand it.

Staplehurst Train Disaster   On 9th June 1865, Dickens experienced a traumatic incident: travelling back from France with Ellen Ternan and her mother, he was involved in a serious railway accident at Staplehurst, in which ten people lost their lives. Dickens was physically unharmed, but nevertheless profoundly affected by it, having spent hours tending the dying and injured with brandy. He drew on the experience in the writing of one of his best short stories, 'The Signalman'.

Final Years   Following the success of his public readings in Britain, Dickens had been contemplating a tour of the United States, and finally embarked on a second trip to America from December 1867 to April 1868. This turned out to be a very lucrative visit, but the exhaustion occasioned by his punishing schedule proved to be disastrous for his health. He began a farewell tour around England in 1868, incorporating a spectacular piece derived from *Oliver Twist*'s scene of Nancy's murder, but was forced to abandon the tour on the instructions of his doctors after he had a stroke in April 1869. Against medical advice, he insisted on giving a series of twelve final readings in London in 1870. These were very well received, many of those who attended commenting that he had never read so well as then. While in London, he had a private audience with Queen Victoria, and met the Prime Minister.

Dickens immersed himself in writing another major novel, *The Mystery of Edwin Drood*, the first six instalments of which were a critical and financial success. Tragically this novel was never to be completed, as Dickens died on 9th June 1870, having suffered a stroke on the previous day. He had wished to be buried in a small graveyard in Rochester, but this was overridden by a nationwide demand that he should be laid to rest in Westminster Abbey. This was done on 14th June 1870, after a strictly private ceremony which he had insisted on in his will.

Death

Charles Dickens's Works

As seen in the account of his life above, Charles Dickens was an immensely prolific writer, not only of novels but of countless articles, sketches, occasional writings and travel accounts, published in newspapers, magazines and in volume form. Descriptions of his most famous works can be found below.

Sketches by Boz, a revised and expanded collection of Dickens's newspaper pieces, was published in two volumes by John Macrone on 8th February 1836. The book was composed of sketches of London life, manners and society. It was an immediate success, and was praised by critics for the "startling fidelity" of its descriptions.

Sketches by Boz

The first instalment of Dickens's first serialized novel, *The Pickwick Papers*, appeared in March 1836. Initially Dickens's contributions were subordinate to those of the illustrator Robert Seymour, but as the series continued, this relationship was inverted, with Dickens's writing at the helm. This led to an upsurge in sales, until *The Pickwick Papers* became a fully fledged literary phenomenon, with circulation rocketing to 40,000 by the final instalment in November 1837. The book centres around the Pickwick Club and its founder, Mr Pickwick, who travels around the country with his companions Mr Winkle, Mr Snodgrass and Mr Tupman, and consists of various loosely connected and light-hearted adventures, with hints of the social satire which would pervade his mature fiction. There is no overall plot, as Dickens invented one episode at a time and, reacting to popular feedback, would switch the emphasis to the most successful characters.

The Pickwick Papers

Oliver Twist   Dickens's first coherently structured novel, *Oliver Twist*, was serialized in *Bentley's Miscellany* from February 1837 to April 1839, with illustrations by the famous caricaturist George Cruikshank. Subtitled *A Parish Boy's Progress*, in reference to Hogarth's *A Rake's Progress* and *A Harlot's Progress* cycles, Dickens tells the story of a young orphan's life and ordeals in London – which had never before been the substance of a novel – as he flees the workhouse and unhappy apprenticeship of his childhood to London, where he falls in with a criminal gang led by the malicious Fagin, before eventually discovering the secret of his origins. *Oliver Twist* publicly addressed issues such as workhouses and child exploitation by criminals – and this preoccupation with social ills and the plight of the downtrodden would become a hallmark of Dickens's fiction.

Nicholas   Dickens's next published novel – the serialization of which
Nickleby   for a while overlapped with that of *Oliver Twist* – was *Nicholas Nickleby*, which revolves around its eponymous hero – again an impoverished young man, though an older one this time – as he tenaciously overcomes the odds to establish himself in the world. When Nicholas's father dies penniless, the family turn to their uncle Ralph Nickleby for assistance, but he turns out to be a mean-spirited miser, and only secures menial positions for Nicholas and his sister Kate. Nicholas is sent to work in Dotheboys Hall, a dreadful Yorkshire boarding school administered by the schoolmaster Wackford Squeers, while Kate endures a humiliating stint at a London millinery. The plot twists and turns until both end up finding love and a secure position in life. Dickens's satire is more trenchant, particularly with regard to Yorkshire boarding schools, which were notorious at the time. Interestingly, within ten years of *Nicholas Nickleby*'s publication all the schools in question were closed down. Overall though, the tone is jovial and the plot is rambling and entertaining, much in the vein of Dickens's eighteenth-century idols Fielding and Smollett.

The Old   *The Old Curiosity Shop* started out as a piece in the short-lived
Curiosity Shop   weekly magazine that Dickens was editing, *Master Humphrey's Clock*, which began publication in April 1840. It was intended to be a miscellany of one-off stories, but as sales were disappointing, Dickens was forced to adapt the 'Personal Adventures of Master Humphrey' into a full-length narrative that would be the most Romantic and fairy-tale-like of Dickens's novels, with some of his greatest humorous passages. The story revolves around Little Nell, a young girl who lives with her grandfather in his eponymous shop, and recounts how the two struggle to release themselves from the grip of the evil usurer dwarf Quilp. By the end of its serialization,

146

circulation had reached the phenomenal figure of 100,000, and Little Nell's death had famously plunged thousands of readers into grief.

As seen above, Dickens took on a different genre for his next major work of fiction, *Barnaby Rudge*: this was a historical novel, addressing the anti-Catholic Gordon riots of 1780, which focused on a village outside London and its protagonist, a simpleton called Barnaby Rudge. The novel was serialized in *Master Humphrey's Clock* from 1840 to 1841, and met with a lukewarm reception from the reading public, who thirsted for more novels in the vein of *The Old Curiosity Shop*. *Barnaby Rudge*

Dickens therefore gave up on the historical genre, and began serializing the more picaresque *Martin Chuzzlewit* from December 1842 to June 1844. The book explores selfishness and its consequences: the eponymous protagonist is the grandson and heir of the wealthy Martin Chuzzlewit senior, and is surrounded by relatives eager to inherit his money. But when Chuzzlewit junior finds himself disinherited and penniless, he has to make his own way in the world. Although it was a step forwards in his writing, being the first of his works to be written with a fully predetermined overall design, it sold poorly – partly due to the fact that publishing in general was experiencing a slump in the early 1840s. In a bid to revive sales, Dickens adjusted the plot during the serialization and sent the title character to America – his own recent visit there providing much material. *Martin Chuzzlewit*

In 1843, Dickens had the idea of writing a small seasonal Christmas book, which would aim to revive the spirit of the holiday and address the social problems that he was increasingly interested in. The resulting work, *A Christmas Carol*, was a phenomenal success at the time, and the tale and its characters, such as Scrooge, Bob Cratchit and Tiny Tim, have now achieved an iconic status. Thackeray famously praised it as "a national benefit and to every man or woman who reads it a personal kindness". Dickens published four more annual Christmas novellas – *The Chimes*, *The Cricket on the Hearth*, *The Battle of Life* and *The Haunted Man* – which were successful at the time, but did not quite live up to the classic appeal of *A Christmas Carol*. After *The Haunted Man*, Dickens discontinued his Christmas books, but he included annual Christmas stories in his magazines *Household Words* and *All the Year Round*. Each set of these stories usually took the form of a miniature *Arabian Nights*, with a number of unrelated short stories linked together through a frame narrative – typically Dickens wrote the frame narrative, and invited other writers to supply the stories included within it, writing the occasional one of them himself. *The Haunted House* appeared in *All the Year Round* in 1862. *Christmas Books and The Haunted House*

Dombey and Son — While living in Lausanne, Dickens composed *Dombey and Son*, which was serialized between October 1846 and April 1848 by Bradbury and Evans with highly successful results. The novel centres on Paul Dombey, the wealthy owner of a shipping company, who desperately wants a son to take over his business after his death. Unfortunately his wife dies giving birth to the longed-for successor, Paul Dombey junior, a sickly child who does not survive long. Although Dombey – who neglects his fatherly responsibilities towards his daughter Florence – is for the most part unsympathetic, he ends up turning a new leaf and becoming a devoted family man. Significantly, this is the first of Dickens's novels for which his working notes survive, from which one can clearly see the great care and detail with which he planned the novel.

David Copperfield — *David Copperfield* (1849–1850) is at once the most personal and the most popular of Dickens's novels. He had tried, probably during 1847–48, to write his autobiography, but, according to his own later account, had found writing about certain aspects, such as his first love for Maria Beadnell, too painful. Instead he chose to transpose autobiographical events into a first-person *Bildungsroman*, *David Copperfield*, which drew on his personal experience of the blacking factory, journalism, his schooling at Wellington House and his love for Maria. Its depiction of the Micawbers owed much to Dickens's own parents. There was great critical acclaim for the novel, and it soon became widely held to be his greatest work.

Bleak House — For his next novel, *Bleak House* (1852–53), Dickens turned his satirical gaze on the English legal system. The focus of the novel is a long-running court case, Jarndyce and Jarndyce, the consequences of which reach from the filthy slums to the landed aristocracy. The scope of the novel may well be the broadest of all of his works, and Dickens also experimented with dual narrators, one in the third person and one in the first. He was well equipped to write on the subject matter due to his experiences as a law clerk and journalist, and his critique of the judiciary system was met with recognition by those involved in it, which helped set the stage for its reform in the 1870s.

Hard Times — *Hard Times* was Dickens's next novel, serialized in *Household Words* between April and August 1854, in which he satirically probed into social and economic issues to a degree not achieved in his other works. Using the infamous characters Thomas Gradgrind and Josiah Bounderby, he attacks utilitarianism, workers' conditions in factories, spurious usage of statistics and fact as opposed to imagination. The story is set in the fictitious northern industrial setting of Coketown, among the workers, school pupils and teachers.

The shortest and most polemical of Dickens's major novels, it sold extremely well on publication, but has only recently been fully accepted into the canon of Dickens's most significant works.

Little Dorrit (1855–57) was also a darkly critical novel, satiriz-   *Little Dorrit*
ing the shortcomings of the government and society, with institu-
tions such as debtor's prisons – in one of which, as seen above,
Dickens's own father had been held – and the fantastically named
Circumlocution Office bearing the brunt of Dickens's bile. The
plot centres on the romance which develops between the characters
of Little Dorrit, a paragon of virtue who has grown up in prison,
and Arthur Clennam, a hapless middle-aged man who returns to
England to make a living for himself after many years abroad.
Although at the time many critics were hostile to the work, taking
issue with what they saw as an overly convoluted plot and a lack
of humour, sales were outstanding and the novel is now ranked as
one of Dickens's finest.

A Tale of Two Cities is the second of Dickens's historical novels,   *A Tale of Two*
covering the period between 1775 and 1793, from the American   *Cities*
Revolution until the middle of the French Revolution. His primary
source was Thomas Carlyle's *The French Revolution*. The story is
of two men – Charles Darnay and Sydney Carton – who look very
similar, though they are utterly different in character, who both
love the same woman, Lucie Manette. The opening and closing
sentences are among the most famous in literature: "It was the best
of times, it was the worst of times." "It is a far, far better thing
that I do, than I have ever done; it is a far, far better rest that I go
to than I have ever known."

Due to a slump in circulation figures for *All the Year Round*,   *Great*
Dickens brought out his next novel, in December 1860, as a weekly   *Expectations*
serial in the magazine, instead of having it published in monthly
instalments as initially intended. The sales promptly recovered,
and the audience and critics were delighted to read the story which
some regard as Dickens's greatest ever work, *Great Expectations*
(1860–61). On publication, it was immediately acclaimed a masterpiece, and was hugely successful in America as well as England.
Like *David Copperfield*, it was written in the first person as a *Bildungsroman*, though this time its protagonist, Pip, was explicitly
working class. Graham Greene once commented: "Dickens had
somehow miraculously varied his tone, but when I tried to analyse
his success, I felt like a colour-blind man trying intellectually to
distinguish one colour from another." George Orwell was moved
to declare: "Psychologically the latter part of *Great Expectations*
is about the best thing Dickens ever did."

Our Mutual Friend

Dickens started work on his next novel, *Our Mutual Friend* (1864–65), by 1861 at the latest. It had an unusually long gestation period, and a mixed reception when first published. However, in recent years it has been reappraised as one of his greatest works. It is probably his most challenging and complicated, although some critics, including G.K. Chesterton, have argued that the ending is rushed. It opens with a young man on his way to receive his inheritance, which he can apparently only attain if he marries a beautiful and mercenary girl, Bella Wilfer, whom he has never met. However, before he arrives, a body is found in the Thames, which is identified as being him. So instead the money passes on to the Boffins, the effects of which spread through to various parts of London society.

The Mystery of Edwin Drood

In April 1870, the first instalment of Dickens's last novel, *The Mystery of Edwin Drood*, appeared. It was the culmination of Dickens's lifelong fascination with murderers. It was favourably received, outselling *Our Mutual Friend*, but only six of the projected twelve instalments were published, as Dickens died in June of that year.

There has naturally been much speculation on how the book would have finished, and suggestions as to how it should end. As it stands, the novel is set in the fictional area of Cloisterham, which is a thinly veiled rendering of Rochester. The plot mainly focuses on the choirmaster and opium addict John Jasper, who is in love with Rosa Bud – his pupil and his nephew Edwin Drood's fiancée. The twins Helena and Neville Landless arrive in Cloisterham, and Neville is attracted to Rosa Bud. Neville and Edwin end up having a huge row one day, after which Neville leaves town, and Edwin vanishes. Neville is questioned about Edwin's disappearance, and John Jasper accuses him of murder.

Select Bibliography

Biographies:
Ackroyd, Peter, *Dickens* (London: Sinclair-Stevenson, 1990)
Forster, John, *The Life of Charles Dickens* (London: Cecil Palmer, 1872–74)
James, Elizabeth, *Charles Dickens* (London: British Library, 2004)
Kaplan, Fred, *Dickens: A Biography* (London: Hodder & Stoughton, 1988)
Smiley, Jane, *Charles Dickens* (London: Weidenfeld and Nicolson, 2002)

Additional Recommended Background Material:
Collins, Philip, ed., *Dickens: The Critical Heritage* (London: Routledge & Kegan Paul, 1971)
Fielding, K.J, *Charles Dickens: A Critical Introduction* 2nd ed. (London: Longmans, 1965)
Wilson, Angus, *The World of Charles Dickens* (London: Secker & Warburg, 1970)

On the Web:
dickens.stanford.edu
dickens.ucsc.edu
www.dickensmuseum.com

ALMA CLASSICS

ALMA CLASSICS aims to publish mainstream and lesser-known European classics in an innovative and striking way, while employing the highest editorial and production standards. By way of a unique approach the range offers much more, both visually and textually, than readers have come to expect from contemporary classics publishing.

LATEST TITLES PUBLISHED BY ALMA CLASSICS

To order any of our titles and for up-to-date information about our current and forthcoming publications, please visit our website on:

www.almaclassics.com